HELIOS CROWNS
HIS MISTRESS

HELIOS CROWNS HIS MISTRESS

BY

MICHELLE SMART

MILLS
BOON

First published in Great Britain 2016
By Mills & Boon, an imprint of HarperCollins*Publishers*
1 London Bridge Street, London, SE1 9GF

Large Print edition 2016

© 2016 Michelle Smart

ISBN: 978-0-263-26199-8

Printed and bound in Great Britain
by CPI Antony Rowe, Chippenham, Wiltshire

This book is for Aimee—thank you for all the support and cheerleading over the years. You're one in a million.

This book is also dedicated to Hannah and Sarah— the mojitos in this are for you!

xxx

CHAPTER ONE

'Do you really have to shave it off?' Amy Green, busy admiring Helios's rear view, slipped a cajoling tone into her plea.

Helios met her eye in the reflection of the bathroom mirror and winked. 'It will grow back.'

She pouted. Carefully. The clay mask she'd applied to her face had dried, making it hard for her to move her features without cracking it. Another ten minutes and she would be able to rinse it off. 'But you're so sexy with a beard.'

'Are you saying I'm not sexy without it?'

She made a harrumphing sound. 'You're always sexy.'

Too sexy for his own good. Even without a beard. Even his voice was sexy: a rich, low-pitched tone that sang to her ears, with the Agon accent which made it dance.

Impossibly tall and rangy, and incredibly strong, with dark olive colouring and ebony hair, currently tousled after a snatched hour in bed with her, Helios had a piratical appearance. The dangerous look was exaggerated by the slight curve of his strong nose and the faint scar running over its bridge: the mark of a fight with his brother Theseus when they were teenagers. Utterly without vanity, Helios wore the scar with pride. He was the sexiest man she'd ever met.

Soon the hair would be tamed and as smooth as his face would be, yet his innate masculinity would still vibrate through him. His rugged body would be hidden by a formal black evening suit, but his strength and vitality would permeate the expensive fabric. The playful expression emanating from his liquid dark brown eyes would still offer sin.

He would turn into Prince Helios Kalliakis, heir to the throne of Agon. But he would still be a flesh and blood man.

He lifted the cut-throat blade. 'Are you sure you don't want to do it?'

Amy shook her head. 'Can you imagine if I were to cut you? I would be arrested for treason.'

He grinned, then gave the mirror a quick wipe

to clear away the condensation produced from the steam of her bath.

Smothering a snigger, she stretched out her right leg until her foot reached the taps, and used her toes to pour a little more hot water in.

'I'm sure deliberately steaming up the bathroom so I can't see properly is also treasonous,' he said with a playful shake of his head, striding lithely to the extractor fan and switching it on.

As with everything in his fabulous palace apartment it worked instantly, clearing the enormous bathroom of steam.

He crouched beside the bath and placed his gorgeous face close to hers. 'Any more treasonous behaviour, *matakia mou*, and I will be forced to punish you.'

His breath, hot and laced with a faint trace of their earlier shared pot of coffee, danced against her skin.

'And what form of punishment will you be forced to give me?' she asked, the desire she'd thought spent bubbling back up inside her, her breaths shortening.

Those liquid eyes flashed and a smirk played on the bowed lips that had kissed her everywhere. It was a mouth a woman could happily kiss for ever.

'A punishment you will never forget.' He snapped his teeth together for effect and growled, before throwing her a look full of promise and striding back to the mirror. Half watching her in the reflection, Helios dipped his shaving brush into the pot and began covering his black beard with a rich, foamy lather.

Amy had to admit watching him shave as if he were the leading man in a medieval film fascinated her. It also scared her. The blade he used was sharp enough to slice through flesh. One twitch of the hand…

All the same, she couldn't drag her eyes away as he scraped the cut-throat razor down his cheek. In its own way it had an eroticism to it, transporting her to a bygone time when men had been *men*. And Helios was all man.

If he wanted he could snap his fingers and an army of courtiers would be there to do the job for him. But that wasn't his style. The Kalliakis family were direct descendants of Ares Patakis, the warrior whose uprising had freed Agon from its Venetian invaders over eight hundred years ago. Agon princes were taught how to wield weapons with the same dedication with which they were taught the art of royal protocol. To her lover, a cut-throat razor was but one of many weapons he'd mastered.

She waited until he'd wiped the blade on a towel to clean it before speaking again. 'Do I take it that despite all my little hints you haven't put a space aside for me tonight?'

Her 'little hints' had taken the form of mentioning at every available opportunity how much she would love to attend the Royal Ball that was the talk of the entire island, but she hadn't seriously expected to get an invitation. She was but a mere employee of the palace museum, and a temporary employee at that.

And it wasn't as if they would be together for ever, she thought with a strange stab of wistfulness. Their relationship had never been a secret, but it hadn't been flaunted either. She was his lover, not his girlfriend, something she had known from the very start. She had no official place in his life and never would.

He placed the blade back to his cheek and swiped, revealing another line of smooth olive skin. 'However much I adore your company, it wouldn't be appropriate for you to attend.'

She pulled a face, inadvertently cracking the mask around her mouth. 'Yes, I know. I am a commoner, and those attending your ball are the *crème de la crème* of high society.'

'Nothing would please me more than to see you there, dressed in the finest haute couture money can buy. But it would be inappropriate for my lover to attend the ball where I'm to select my future wife.'

The deliciously warm bath turned cold in the beat of a moment.

She sat up.

'Your future wife? What are you talking about?'

His reflected eyes met hers again. 'The underlying reason for this ball is so that I can choose a wife.'

She paused before asking, 'Like in *Cinderella*?'

'Exactly.' He worked on his chin, then wiped the blade on the towel again. 'You know all of this.'

'No,' she said slowly, her blood freezing to

match the chills rippling over her skin. 'I was under the impression this ball was a pre-Gala do.'

In three weeks the eyes of the world would be on Agon as the island celebrated fifty years of King Astraeus's reign. Heads of state and dignitaries from all around the world would be flying in for the occasion.

'And so it is. I think the phrase is "killing two birds with one stone"?'

'Why can't you find a wife in the normal way?' And, speaking of normal, how were her vocal cords performing when the rest of her body had been subsumed in a weird kind of paralysis?

'Because, *matakia mou*, I am heir to the throne. I have to marry someone of royal blood. You know that.'

Yes, that she *did* know. Except she hadn't thought it would be now. It hadn't occurred to her. Not once. Not while they were sharing a bed every night.

'I need to choose wisely,' he continued, speaking in the same tone he might use if he were discussing what to order from the palace kitchen for dinner. 'Obviously I have a shortlist of preferred women—princesses and duchesses I have met through the years who have caught my attention.'

'Obviously…' she echoed. 'Is there any particular woman at the top of your shortlist, or are there a few of them jostling for position?'

'Princess Catalina of Monte Cleure is looking the most likely. I've known her and her family for years—they've attended our Christmas Balls since Catalina was a baby. Her sister and brother-in-law got together at the last one.' He grinned at the scandalous memory. 'Catalina and I dined together a couple of times when I was in Denmark the other week. She has all the makings of an excellent queen.'

An image of the raven-haired Princess, a famed beauty who dealt with incessant press scrutiny on account of her ethereal royal loveliness, came to Amy's mind. Waves of nausea rolled in her belly.

'You never mentioned it.'

'There was nothing to say.' He didn't look the slightest bit shamefaced.

'Did you sleep with her?'

He met her stare, censure clear in his reflection. 'What kind of a question is *that*?'

'A natural question for a woman to ask her lover.'

Until that moment it hadn't been something that had occurred to her: the idea that he might have strayed. Helios had never promised fidelity, but he hadn't needed to. Since their first night together their lust for each other had been all-consuming.

'The Princess is a virgin and will remain one until her wedding day whether she marries me or some other man. Does that answer your question?'

Not even a little bit. All it did was open up a whole heap of further questions, all of which she didn't have the right to ask and not one of which she wanted to hear the answer to.

The only question she *could* bring herself to ask was 'When are you hoping to marry the lucky lady?'

If he heard the irony in her voice he hid it well. 'It will be a state wedding, but I would hope to be married in a couple of months.'

A couple of months? He expected to choose a

bride and have a state wedding in a few months? Surely it wasn't possible…?

But this was Helios. If there was one thing she knew about her lover it was that he was not a man to let the grass grow beneath his feet. If he wanted something done he wanted it done now, not tomorrow.

But a couple of months…?

Amy was contracted to stay in Agon until September, which was five whole months away. She'd imagined… Hoped…

She thought of King Astraeus, Helios's grand-father. She had never met the King, but through her work in the palace museum she felt she had come to know him. The King was dying. Helios needed to marry and produce an heir of his own to assure the family line.

She *knew* all this. Yet still she'd shared his bed night after night and allowed herself to believe that Helios would hold off his wedding until her time on Agon was up.

Gripping the sides of the free-standing bath, she got carefully to her feet and stepped out. Hands trembling, she pulled a warm, fluffy towel off the rack and held it to her chest, not wanting to waste a second, not even to wrap it around herself.

Helios pulled his top lip down and brought the blade down in careful but expert fashion. 'I'll call you when the ball is finished.'

She strode to the door, uncaring that bathwater was dripping off her and onto the expensive floor tiles. 'No, you won't.'

'Where are you going? You're soaking wet.'

From out of the corner of her eye she saw him pat his towel over his face and follow her through into his bedroom, not bothering to cover himself.

She gathered her clothes into a bundle and held them tightly. A strange burning buzzed in her brain, making coherent thought difficult.

Three months. That was how long she'd shared his bed. In that time they'd slept apart on only a dozen or so occasions, when Helios had been away on official business. Like when he'd gone to Denmark and, unbeknownst to her, dined with Princess Catalina. And now he was throwing a ball to find the woman he would share a bed with for the rest of his life.

She'd known from the start that they had no future, and had been careful to keep her heart and emotions detached. But to hear him being so blasé about it…

She stood by the door that opened into the secret passageway connecting their apartments. There were dozens and dozens of such secret passageways throughout the palace; a fortress built on intrigue and secrets.

'I'm going to my apartment. Enjoy your evening.'

'Have I missed something?'

The fact that he looked genuinely perplexed only made matters worse.

'You say it isn't appropriate for me to come tonight, but I'll tell you what isn't appropriate— talking about the wife you're hours away from selecting with the woman who has shared your bed for three months.'

'I don't know what your problem is,' he said with a shrug, raising his hands in an open-palmed gesture. 'My marriage won't change anything between us.'

'If you believe that then you're as stupid as you are insensitive and misogynistic. You speak as if the women you are selecting from are sweets lined up in a shop rather than flesh and blood people.' She shook her head to emphasise her distaste, watching as her words seeped in and the perplexity on Helios's face darkened into something ugly.

Helios was not a man who received criticism well. On this island and in this palace he was celebrated and feted, a man whose words people hung on to. Affable and charming, his good humour was infectious. Cross him, however, and he would turn with the snap of two fingers.

If she wasn't so furious with him Amy would probably be afraid.

He strode towards her, magnificently naked. He stopped a foot away and folded his arms across his defined chest. A pulse throbbed at his temple and his jaw clenched tightly.

'Be careful in how you speak to me. I might be your lover, but you do not have a licence to insult me.'

'Why? Because you're a prince?' She hugged the towel and the bundle of clothes even tighter, as if their closeness could stop her erratically thumping heart from jumping out of her chest. 'You're about to make a commitment to another woman and I want no part of it.'

Benedict, Helios's black Labrador, sensed the atmosphere and padded over to her, his tongue lolling out as he sat on his haunches by her side and gave what looked like a disapproving stare at his master.

Helios noticed it too. He rubbed Benedict's head, the darkness disappearing as quickly as it had appeared, an indulgent smile spreading over his face as he looked at Amy. 'Don't be so dramatic. I know you're premenstrual, and that makes you more emotional than you would otherwise be, but you're being irrational.'

'Premenstrual? Did you really just say that? You really are on a different planet. God forbid that I should become "emotional" because my lover has had secret dates with other women and is about to take one of them for his wife and still expects me to warm his bed. But don't worry. Pat me on the head and tell me I'm premenstrual. Pat yourself on the back and tell yourself you've done nothing wrong.'

Too furious to look at him any more, she turned the handle of the door and pushed it open with her hip.

'Are you walking away from me?'

Was that *laughter* in his voice? Did he find this *amusing*?

Ignoring him, Amy raised her head high and walked up the narrow passageway that would take her to her own palace apartment.

A huge hand gripped her biceps, forcing her to twist around. He absolutely dwarfed her.

Regardless of the huge tug in her heart and the rising nausea, her voice was steady as she said, 'Get your hands off me. We're over.'

'No, we're not.' He slid his hand over her shoulder to snake it around her neck. His breath was hot in her ear as he leaned down to whisper, 'While you're sulking tonight I will be thinking of you and imagining all the ways I can take you when the ball's over. Then you will come to me and we will act them all out.'

Despite her praying to all the gods she could think of, her body reacted to his words and to his closeness the way it always did. With Helios she was like a starved child, finally allowed to feast. She craved him. She had desired him from the moment she'd met him all those months ago, with a powerful need that hadn't abated with time.

But now the time had come to conquer the craving.

Pressing a hand to his solid chest, resisting the urge to run her fingers through the fine black hair that covered it, she pushed herself back and forced her eyes to meet his still playful gaze.

'Enjoy your evening. Try not to spill wine down any princess's dress.'

His mocking laughter followed her all the way to the sanctuary of her own apartment.

It wasn't until she arrived in her apartment, which was spacious compared to normal accommodation but tiny when compared to Helios's, and caught a glimpse of her reflection that she saw the clay mask was still on her face.

It had cracked all over.

Helios led his dance partner—a princess from the old Greek royal family—around the ballroom. She was a very pretty young woman, but as he danced with her and listened to her chatter he mentally struck her off his list. Whoever he married, he wanted to be able to hold a conversation with them about something other than the latest catwalk fashions.

When the waltz had finished he bowed gracefully and excused himself to join his brother Theseus at his table, ignoring all the pleading female eyes silently begging him to take their hand next.

Amy's words about him treating the women here as sweets in a shop came back to him. He was man enough to admit they held the ring of truth. But if he had to choose someone to spend the rest of his life with and to bear his children, he wanted a woman as close to being perfect on his palate as he could taste.

If Amy could see the ladies in question and their eager eyes, the way they thrust their cleavages in his direction as they passed him, hoping to garner his attention, she would understand that they *wanted* to be tasted. They wanted him to find them exactly to his taste.

Theseus's gaze was directed at their younger brother, Talos, who was dancing with the ravishing violinist who would play at their grandfather's Jubilee Gala in three weeks.

'There's something going on there,' Theseus said, swigging back his champagne. 'Look at him. The fool's smitten.'

Helios followed his brother's gaze to the dance floor and knew immediately what he meant. The other couple of hundred guests in the room might as well not have been there for all the attention Talos and his dance partner were paying them. They had eyes only for each other and the heat they were producing…it was almost a visible entity. And strangely mesmerising.

Not for the first time Helios wished Amy could be there. She would adore waltzing around the great ballroom. For a conscientious academic she had a fun side that made her a pleasure to be with.

Theseus fixed his gaze back on Helios. 'So what about you? Shouldn't you be on the dance floor?'

'I'm taking a breather.'

'You should be taking it with Princess Catalina.'

Helios and his brothers had discussed his potential brides numerous times. The consensus was that Catalina would be a perfect fit for their family.

Only a generation ago, the marriages of the heirs to the Agon throne had been arranged. His own parents' marriage had been arranged. It had been witnessing the implosion of their marriage that had led his grandfather King Astraeus to abandon protocol and allow the next generation to select their own spouses, providing they were of royal blood.

For this, Helios was grateful. He was determined that whoever he selected would have no illusions that their marriage would be anything but one of duty.

'You think...?' he asked idly, while his skin crawled at the thought of dancing another waltz with any more of the ladies in attendance, no matter how beautiful they were. Beautiful women were freely available wherever he went. Women of substance less so.

He glanced at his watch. Another couple of hours and this would be over. He would call Amy and she would come to him.

Now, *she* was a woman of substance.

A frisson of tension raced through him as he recalled their earlier exchange. He'd never seen her angry before. There'd been a possessiveness to that anger too. She'd been jealous.

Usually when a lover showed the first sign of

possessiveness it meant it was time for him to move on. In Amy's case he'd found it highly alluring. Her jealousy had strangely delighted him.

Helios had long suspected that she kept parts of herself hidden from him. She gave her body to him willingly, and revelled in their lovemaking as much as he did, but the inner workings of her clever mind remained a mystery.

She'd been different from his usual lovers from the very start. Beautiful and fiercely intelligent, she held his attention in a way no other woman ever had. Her earlier anger hadn't repelled him, as it would have done coming from anyone else; it had intrigued him, peeling away another layer of the brilliant, passionate woman he couldn't get enough of. When he was with her he could forget everything and live for the moment, for their hunger.

The seriousness of his grandfather's illness clung to him like a barnacle, but when he was with Amy it became tamed, was less of a thudding beat of pain and doom. When he was with her he could cast aside the great responsibilities being heir to the throne brought and simply be a man. A lover. *Her* lover. She was a constant thrum in his blood. He had no intention of giving her up—marriage or no marriage.

'Has anyone else caught your attention?' Theseus asked him.

'No.'

Helios had always known he would have to marry. There had never been any question about it. He had no personal feelings about it one way or another. Marriage was an institution within which to produce the next set of Kalliakis heirs, and he was fortunate to be in a position where he could choose his own bride, albeit within certain constraints. His parents hadn't been so lucky. Their marriage had been arranged before his mother had been out of nappies. It had been a disaster. His only real hope for his own marriage was that it be *nothing* like theirs.

Princess Catalina, currently dancing with a British prince, caught his eye. She really was incredibly beautiful. Refined. Her breeding and lineage shone through. Her brother was an old school friend of his, and their meals together in Denmark had shown her to be a woman of great intelligence as well as beauty, if a little serious for his taste.

She had none of Amy's irreverence.

Still, Catalina would make an excellent queen and he'd wasted enough time as it was. He should have selected a wife months ago, when the gravity of his grandfather's condition had been spelt out to him and his brothers.

Catalina had been raised in a world of protocol, just as he had. She had no illusions or expectations of love. If he chose her he knew theirs would be a marriage of duty. Nothing more, nothing less. No emotional entanglements. Exactly as he wanted.

Making a family with her would be no hardship either. He was certain that with some will on both their parts a bond would form. Chemistry should ensue too. Not the same kind of chemistry he shared with Amy, of course. That would be impossible to replicate.

A memory of Amy heading barefoot down the dimly lit passageway, her clothes and towel huddled to her, her dark blonde hair damp and swinging across her golden back, her bare bottom swaying, flashed into his mind. She'd been as haughty as any princess in that moment, and he couldn't wait to punish her for her insolence.

He would bring her to the brink of orgasm so many times she would be *begging* him for release.

But this was neither the time nor the place to imagine Amy's slender form naked in his arms.

With titanium will, he dampened down the fire spreading through his loins and fixed his attention on the women before him. For the next few hours Amy had to be locked away in his mind to free up his concentration for the job in hand.

Before he could bring himself to dance again he beckoned a footman closer, so he could take another glass of champagne and drink a large swallow.

Theseus eyed him shrewdly. 'What's the matter with you?'

'Nothing.'

'You have the face of a man at a wine-tasting event discovering all the bottles are corked.'

Helios fixed a smile on his face. 'Better?'

'Now you look like a mass murderer.'

'Your support is, as always, invaluable.' Draining his glass, he got to his feet. 'Considering the fact I'm not the only Prince expected to marry and produce heirs, I suggest you get off your backside and mingle with the beautiful ladies in attendance too.'

He smirked at Theseus's grimace. While Helios accepted his fate with the steely backbone his upbringing and English boarding school education had instilled in him, he knew his rebellious brother looked forward to matrimony with all the enthusiasm of a zebra entering a lion enclosure.

Later, as he danced with Princess Catalina, holding her at a respectable distance so their bodies didn't touch—and having no compulsion to bridge the gap—his thoughts turned to his grandfather.

The King was not in attendance tonight, as he was saving his limited energy for the Jubilee Gala itself. It was for that great man, who had raised Helios and his brothers since Helios was ten, that he was prepared to take the final leap and settle down.

For his grandfather he would do *anything*.

Soon the crown would pass to him—sooner than he had wanted or expected—and he needed a queen by his side. He wanted his grandfather to move on to the next life at peace, in the knowledge that the succession of the Kalliakis line was secure. If time was kind to them his grandfather might just live long enough to see Helios take his vows.

CHAPTER TWO

WHERE THE HELL was she?

Helios had been back in his apartment for fifteen minutes and Amy wasn't answering his calls. According to the head of security, she had left the palace. Her individual passcode showed that she'd left at seven forty-five; around the time he and his brothers had been welcoming their guests.

Trying her phone one more time, he strolled through to his bar and poured himself a large gin. The call went straight to voicemail. He tipped the neat liquid down his throat and, on a whim, carried the bottle through to his study.

Security monitors there showed pictures from the cameras that ran along the connecting passageways. Only Helios himself had access to the cameras' feeds.

He peered closely at the screen for camera three, which faced the reinforced connecting door. There was something on the floor he couldn't make out clearly...

Striding to it and unbolting the door, he stared down at a box. Crammed inside were bottles of perfume, jewellery, books and mementos. All the gifts he had given Amy during their time together as lovers. Crammed, unwanted, into a box and left on his doorstep.

A burst of fury tore through him, so sudden and so powerful it consumed him in one.

Before he had time to think what he was doing he raised his foot and brought it slamming down onto the box. Glass shattered and crunched beneath him, the sound echoing in the silence.

For an age he did nothing else but inhale deeply, trembling with fury, fighting the urge to smash what was left of the box's contents into smithereens. Violence had been his father's solution to life's problems. It was something Helios had always known resided inside him too but, unlike in his father's case, it was an aspect of himself he controlled.

The sudden fury that had just overtaken him was incomprehensible.

* * *

Acutely aware of how late she was, Amy slammed her apartment door shut and hurried down the stairs that led to the palace museum. Punching in her passcode, she waited for the green light to come on, shoved the door open and stepped into the private quarters of the museum, an area out of bounds to visitors.

Gazing longingly at the small staff kitchen as she passed it, she crossed her fingers in the hope that the daily pastries hadn't already been eaten and the coffee already drunk. The *bougatsas*, freshly made by the palace chefs and brought to them every morning, had become her favourite food in the whole world.

Her mouth filled with moisture as she imagined the delicate yet satisfying filo-based pastries. She hoped there were still some custard-filled ones left. She'd hardly eaten a thing in the past couple of days, and now, after finally managing to get a decent night's sleep, she'd woken up ravenous. She'd also slept right through her alarm clock, and the thought made her legs work even quicker as she climbed another set of stairs that led up to the boardroom.

'I'm so sorry I'm late,' she said, rushing through the door, a hand flat on her breathless chest. 'I over…' Her words tailed off as she saw Helios, sitting at the head of the large round table.

His elbows rested on the table, the tips of his fingers rubbing together. He was freshly shaven and, even casually dressed as he was, in a dark green long-sleeved crew-neck top, he exuded an undeniable power. And all the force of that power was at that very moment aimed at her.

'Nice of you to join us, Despinis Green,' he said. His tone was even, but his dark brown eyes resembled bullets waiting to be fired at her. 'Take a seat.'

Utterly shaken to see him there, she blinked rapidly and forced herself to inhale. Helios was the palace museum's director, but his involvement in the day-to-day running of it was minimal. In the four months she'd worked there, he hadn't once attended the weekly Tuesday staff meeting.

She'd known when she'd stolen back into the palace late last night that she would have to face him soon, but she'd hoped for a few more days' grace. Why did he have to appear today, of all days? The one time she'd overslept and looked awful.

Unfortunately the only chair available was directly opposite him. It made a particularly loud scraping sound over the wooden floor as she pulled it back and sat down, clasping her hands tightly on her lap so as not to betray their tremors. Greta, one of the other curators and Amy's best friend on the island, had the seat next to her. She placed a comforting hand over hers and squeezed gently. Greta knew everything.

In the centre of the table was the tray of *bougatsas* Amy had hoped for. Three remained, but she found her appetite gone and her heart thundering so hard that the ripples spread to her belly and made her nauseous.

Greta poured her a cup of coffee. Amy clutched it gratefully.

'We were discussing the artefacts we're still waiting on for my grandfather's exhibition,' Helios said, looking directly at her.

The Agon Palace Museum was world-famous, and as such attracted curators from across the world, resulting in a medley of first languages amongst the staff. To simplify matters, English was the official language spoken when on duty.

Amy cleared her throat and searched her scrambled brain for coherence. 'The marble statues are on their way from Italy as we speak and should arrive in port early tomorrow morning.'

'Do we have staff ready to welcome them?'

'Bruno will message me when they reach Agon waters,' she said, referring to one of the Italian curators accompanying the statues back to their homeland. 'As soon as I hear from him we'll be ready to go. The drivers are on call. Everything is in hand.'

'And what about the artefacts from the Greek museum?'

'They will arrive here on Friday.'

Helios *knew* all this. The exhibition was his pet project and they'd worked closely together on it.

She'd first come to Agon in November, as part of a team from the British Museum delivering artefacts on loan to the Agon Palace Museum. During those few days on the island she'd struck up a friendship with Pedro, the Head of Museum. Unbeknownst to her at the time, he'd been impressed with her knowledge of Agon, and doubly impressed with her PhD thesis on Minoan Heritage and its Influences on Agon Culture. Pedro had been the one to suggest her for the role of curator for the Jubilee Exhibition.

The offer had been a dream come true, and a huge honour for someone with so little experience. Only twenty-seven, what Amy lacked in experience she made up for with enthusiasm.

Amy had learned at the age of ten that the happy, perfect family she'd taken for granted was not as she'd been led to believe. *She* wasn't what she'd been led to believe. Her dad was indeed her biological father, but her brothers were only half-brothers. Her mum wasn't her biological mother. The woman who'd actually given birth to her had been from the Mediterranean island of Agon.

Half of Amy's DNA was Agonite.

Since that bombshell discovery, everything about Agon had fascinated her. She'd devoured books on its Minoan history and its evolution into democracy. She'd thrilled at stories of the wars, the passion and ferocity of its people. She'd studied maps and photographs, staring so intently at the island's high green mountains, sandy beaches and clear blue seas that its geography had become as familiar as her own home town.

Agon had been an obsession.

Somewhere in its history was *her* history, and the key to understanding who she truly was. To have the opportunity to live there on a nine-month secondment had been beyond anything she could have hoped. It had been as if fate was giving her the push she needed to find her birth mother. Somewhere in this land of half a million people was the woman who had borne her.

For seventeen years Amy had thought about her, wondering what she looked like—did she look like *her*?—what her voice sounded like, what regrets she might have. Was she ashamed of what she'd done? Surely she was? How could anyone live through what Neysa Soukis had done and *not* feel shame?

She'd been easy to locate, but how to approach her…? That had always been the biggest question. Amy couldn't just turn up at her door; it would likely be slammed in her face and then she would never have her answers. She'd considered writing a letter but had failed to think of what she could say other than: *Hi, do you re-member me? You carried me for nine months and then dumped me. Any chance you could tell me why?*

Greek social media, which Greta had been helping her with, had proved fruitful. Neysa didn't use it, but through it Amy had discov-ered a half-brother. Tentative communications had started between them. She had to hope he would act as a conduit between them.

'Have you arranged transport for Friday?' Helios asked, the dark eyes hard, the bowed, sensual mouth tight.

'Yes. Everything is in hand,' she said for a sec-ond time, as a sharp pang reached through her as she realised she would never feel those lips on hers again. 'We're ahead of schedule.'

'You're confident that come the Gala the ex-hibition will be ready?'

His voice was casual but there was a hardness there, a scepticism she'd never had directed at her before.

'Yes,' she answered, gritting her teeth to stop her hurt and anger leeching out.

He was punishing her. She should have answered one of his calls. She'd taken the coward's way out and escaped from the palace in the hope that a few days away from him would give her the strength she needed to resist him. The best way—the only way—of beating her craving for him would be by going cold turkey.

Because resist him she must. She couldn't be the other woman. She couldn't.

But she hadn't imagined that seeing him again would physically *hurt*.

It did. Dreadfully.

Before her job had been rubber-stamped, Helios had interviewed her himself. The Jubilee Exhibition was of enormous personal importance to him and he'd been determined that the curator with the strongest affinity to his island would get the job.

Luckily for her, he'd agreed with Pedro that she was the perfect candidate. He'd told her some months later, when they'd been lying replete in each other's arms, that it had been her passion and enthusiasm that had convinced him. He'd known she would give the job the dedication it deserved.

Meeting Helios… He'd been *nothing* as she'd

imagined: as far from the stuffy, pompous, 'entitled' Prince she'd expected him to be as was possible.

Her attraction to him had been immediate, a chemical reaction over which she'd had no control. It had taken her completely off guard. Yet she hadn't thought anything of it. He was a prince, after all, both powerful and dangerously handsome. Never in her wildest dreams had she thought the attraction would be reciprocated. But it had been.

He'd been much more involved with the exhibition than she'd anticipated, and she'd often found herself working alone with him, her longing for him an ever-growing fire inside her that she didn't have a clue how to handle.

Affairs in the workplace were a fact of life, even in the studious world of antiquities, but they were not something she'd ever been tempted by. She loved her work so much it took her entire focus. Her work gave her purpose. It grounded her. And working with the ancient objects of her own people, seeing first-hand how techniques and social mores had evolved over the years, was a form of proof that the past didn't have to be the future. Her birth mother's actions didn't have to define her, even if she did feel the taint of her behaviour like an invisible stain.

Relationships of any real meaning had always been out of the question for her. How could she commit to someone if she didn't know who she truly was? So to find herself feeling such an attraction, and to the man who was effectively her boss, who just happened to be a prince... It was no wonder her emotions had been all over the place.

Helios had had no such inhibitions.

Long before he'd laid so much as a finger on her he'd undressed her with his dark liquid eyes, time and again. Until one late afternoon, when she'd been talking to him in the smaller of the exhibition rooms, she on one side, he on the other, and he'd gone from complete stillness to fluid motion in the beat of a heart. He'd walked to her with long strides and pulled her into his arms.

And that had been it. She'd been his for the taking. And he'd been hers.

Their three months together had been a dream. Theirs had been a physically intense but surpris-

ingly easy relationship. There had been no expectations. No inhibitions. Just passion.

Walking away should have been easy.

The eyes that had undressed her a thousand
times now flickered to Pedro, giving silent per-
mission for him to move the discussion on to
general museum topics. There might be a special
exhibition being organised, but the museum itself still needed to be run to its usual high standards.

Clearly unnerved—Helios's mood, usually so
congenial, was unsettling all the staff—Pedro
raced through the rest of the agenda in dou-
ble-quick time, finally mentioning the need for
someone to cover for one of their tour guides
that Thursday. Amy was happy to volunteer.
Thursday was her only reasonably quiet day
that week, and she enjoyed taking on the tours
whenever the opportunity arose.

One of the things she loved so much about the
museum was the collaborative way it was run,
with everyone helping each other when needed.
It was a philosophy that came from the very top,
from Helios himself, even if today there was no
sign of his usual amiability.

Only at the very end of the meeting did Pedro say, 'Before we leave, can I remind everyone that menus for next Wednesday need to be handed in by Friday?'

As a thank-you for all the museum staff's hard work in organising the exhibition, Helios had arranged a night out for everyone before the summer rush hit, all expenses paid. It was a typically generous gesture from him, and a social event Amy had been very much looking forward to. Now, though, the thought of a night out with Helios in attendance made her stomach twist.

There was a palpable air of relief when the meeting finished. Today there was none of the usual lingering. Everyone scrambled to their feet and rushed for the door.

'Amy, a word please.' Helios's rich voice rose over the clatter of hurrying feet.

She paused, inches from the door, inches from escape. Arranging her face into a neutral expression, she turned around.

'Shut the door behind you.'

She did as she was told, her heart sinking to her feet, then sat back in her original place op-

posite him but also the greatest distance possible away.

It wasn't far enough.

The man oozed testosterone.

He also oozed menace.

Her heart kicked against her ribs. She clamped
her lips together and folded her arms across her
chest.

Yet she couldn't stop her eyes moving to his,
couldn't stop herself gazing at him.

His silver chain glinted against the base of his
throat. That chain had often brushed against her
lips when he'd made love to her.

And as she stared at him, wondering when he
was going to speak, his eyes studied her with the
same intensity, making her mouth run dry and
her hammering pulse race into a gallop.

His fingers drummed on the table. 'Did you
have a nice time at Greta's?'

'Yes, thank you,' she replied stiffly, before she
realised what he'd said. 'How did you know I
was there?'

'Through the GPS on your phone.'

'What? You've been *spying* on me?'

'You are the lover of the heir to the throne of

Agon. Our relationship is an open secret. I do not endanger what is mine.'

'I'm not yours. Not any more,' she spat at him, running from fear to fury in seconds. 'Whatever tracking device you've put in my phone, you can take it out. Now.'

She yanked her bag onto the table, pulled out her phone and threw it at him.

His hand opened to catch it like a Venus fly-trap catching its prey. He laughed. But unlike on Saturday, when he'd thought he'd been indulging her, the sound contained no humour.

He slid the phone back to her. 'There's no tracking device in it. It's all done through your number.'

'Well, you can damn well *un*track it. Take it off your system, or whatever it's on.'

He studied her contemplatively. His stillness unnerved her. Helios was *never* still. He had enough energy to power the whole palace.

'Why did you leave?'

'To get away from you.'

'You didn't think I would be worried?'

'I thought you'd be too busy cherry-picking your bride to notice I'd gone.'

Finally a smile played on his lips. 'Ah, so you were punishing me.'

'No, I was not,' she refuted hotly. 'I was giving myself space away from you because I knew you'd still expect to sleep with me after an evening of wooing prospective brides.'

'And you didn't think you'd be able to resist me?'

Her cheeks coloured and Helios felt a flare of satisfaction that his thoughts had been correct.

His beautiful, passionate lover had been jealous.

Slender, feminine to her core, with a tumbling mane of thick dark blonde hair, Amy was possibly the most beautiful woman he'd ever met. A sculptor wouldn't hesitate to cast her as Aphrodite. She made his blood thicken just to look at her, even dressed as she was now in an A-line navy skirt and a pretty yet demure lilac top.

But today there was something unkempt about her appearance that wasn't usually there: dark hollows beneath her taupe eyes, her rosebud lips dry, her usual glowing complexion paler than was normal.

And he was the cause of it. The thought sent

a thrill through him. Whatever punishment she had hoped to inflict on him by disappearing for a few days, it had backfired on her.

He would never let her know of the overwhelming fury that had rent him when he'd seen the box she'd left by his door.

Which reminded him…

He slid the thick padded envelope he'd placed on the table towards her. Smashing the box when his anger had got the better of him had caused the perfume bottles to spill and ruin the books, but the jewellery had been left undamaged.

Her eyes narrowed with caution, she extended an elegant hand to it and opened it gingerly. Her mouth tightened when she saw what was inside.

She dropped the envelope back on the table and got quickly to her feet. 'I don't want them.'

'They're yours. You insult me by returning them.'

She didn't blink. 'And you insult me by giving them back when you're about to put an engagement ring on another woman's finger.'

He got out of his chair and stalked over to her. With the chair behind her she had nowhere to retreat. He pulled her to him, enfolding her in his arms so that her head was pressed to his chest. He was too strong and she was too slender for her to wriggle out of his hold, and in any case he knew her attempts didn't mean anything.

He could feel her heat. She *wanted* to be in his arms.

Her head was tilted back, her breaths quickening. He watched as the pupils of her eyes darkened and pulsed, as the grey turned to brown, with a passionate fury there that set his veins alight.

'There is no need to be jealous,' he murmured, pressing himself closer. 'My marriage doesn't change my feelings for you.'

Her left eye twitched, an affliction he'd never seen before. Her top teeth razed across her full bottom lip.

'But it changes my feelings for you.'

'Liar. You can't deny you still want me.' He brushed his cheek against hers and whispered into her ear, 'Only a few days ago you screamed out my name. I still have your scratches on my back.'

She reared back. 'That was before I knew you

were looking for an immediate wife. I will not be your mistress.'

'There is no shame in it. Generations of Agon monarchs have taken lovers after marriage.' His grandfather had been the exception to the rule, but only because he'd been fortunate enough to fall in love with his wife.

Of the thirty-one monarchs who'd ruled Agon since 1203, only a handful had found love and fidelity with their spouses. His own father, although he'd died before he could take the throne, had had dozens of lovers and mistresses. He'd revelled in waving his indiscretions right under his loving wife's nose.

'And generations ago your ancestors chopped your enemies' limbs off but you've managed to wean yourself off that.'

He laughed at her retort, running a finger over her chin. Even with her oval face free of make-up Amy was beautiful. 'We don't marry for love or companionship, as other people do. We marry for the good of our island. Think of it as a business arrangement. *You* are my lover. You are the woman I *want* to be with.'

His mother had been unfortunate in that she'd

already loved his father when they had married, and it was that love which had ultimately destroyed her, long before the car crash that had taken both his parents' lives.

He would never inflict the kind of pain his father had caused, not on anyone. He had to marry, but he was upfront about what he wanted: a royal wife to produce the next generation of Kalliakis heirs. No emotions. No expectations of fidelity. A union founded on duty and nothing more.

Amy stared at him without speaking for the longest time, searching for something. He didn't know what she hoped to find.

He brought his face down to meet her lips, which had parted, but she pulled back so only the faintest of touches passed between them.

'I mean it, Helios. We're finished. I will never be your mistress.' Her words were but a whisper.

'You think?'

'Yes.'

'Then why are you still standing here? Why is your breath still warm on my face?'

Brushing his lips across the softness of her cheek, he gripped her bottom and ground her against him, letting her feel his desire for her. The tiniest of moans escaped her throat.

'See?' He trailed kisses over her delicate ear. 'You do want me. But you're punishing me.'

'No, I…'

'Shh…' He placed a finger on her mouth. 'We both know I could take you right now and you would welcome it.'

Heat flared from her eyes but her chin jutted up mutinously.

'I am going to give you exactly five seconds of freedom. Five seconds to leave this room. If after those five seconds you are still here…' he spoke very quietly into her ear '…I will lift up your skirt and make love to you right here and now on this table.'

She quivered, a small tell but one so familiar he knew the expression that would be in her eyes when he looked into them.

He was right. The taupe had further darkened; the pupils were even more dilated. The tip of her pink tongue glistened between her parted lips. He knew that if he placed his hands over her small but beautifully formed breasts he would feel her nipples strain towards him.

He released his hold on her and folded his arms across his chest.

'One.'

She put a hand to her mouth and dragged it down over her chin.

'Two.'

She swallowed. Her eyes never left his face. He could practically smell her longing.

'Three... Four...'

She turned on her heel and fled to the door.

'One week,' he called to her retreating back. She was halfway out of the room and made no show of listening to him, but he knew she heard every word. 'One week and you, *matakia mou*, will be back in my bed. I guarantee it.'

CHAPTER THREE

AMY GAZED AT the marble statues that had arrived on Agon by ship that morning and now sat in the grand entrance hall of the museum on their plinths. Three marble statues. Three kings at the height of their glory. All named Astraeus. The fourth, specially commissioned for the exhibition, would be transported from the sculptor's studio in a week's time. It would depict the current monarch, the fourth King Astraeus, as a young man in his prime.

Helios had personally commissioned it. She didn't want to think of Helios. But she couldn't stop.

He was everywhere. In every painting, every sculpture, every fragment of framed scripture, every piece of pottery. Everything was a reminder that this was all his. His people. His ancestors. Him.

Her attention kept flickering back to the statue

of the second King Astraeus, a marble titan dating from 1403. Trident in hand and unashamedly naked, he had the same arrogant look with an underlying hint of ferociousness that Helios carried so well. If she had known nothing of the Agon royal dynasty, she would have known instinctively that her lover was a descendent of this man. Agon had been at peace for decades but their warrior roots dated back millennia, were ingrained in their DNA.

Helios had warrior roots in spades.

She had to stop thinking about him.

God, this was supposed to be easy. An affair with no promises and no need for compromise.

She'd been so tempted to stay in the boardroom with him. She'd *ached* to stay. Her body had been weighted down with need for him. But in the back of her mind had been an image of him exchanging his vows with a faceless woman who would become his wife.

Amy couldn't be the other woman. Whatever kind of marriage Helios had in mind for himself, it would still be real. He needed an heir. He would make love to his wife.

She could never allow herself to be the cause

of pain and humiliation in another. She'd seen first-hand the damage an affair could cause. After all, she was the result of an affair herself. She'd spent seventeen years knowing she was the result of something sordid.

She was nothing but a dirty secret.

Helios's driver brought the car to a stop at the back of the palace, beside his private entrance. Dozens and dozens of schoolchildren of all shapes and sizes were picnicking on the lawn closest to the museum entrance: some playing football, some doing cartwheels and handstands. In the far distance a group were filing out of the Agon palace's maze, which was famed as one of the biggest and tallest mazes in the world.

Helios checked the time. He was always too busy to spend as much time with the palace visitors as he would like.

He had a small window before he was due at a business meeting he'd arranged with his brothers. His brothers ran the day-to-day side of their investment business, but he was still heavily involved. Then there were his royal duties, which had increased exponentially since the onset of his grandfather's illness. He was in all but name Prince Regent, the highest ranking ambassador for his beloved island. It was his duty to do everything he could to bring investment and tourists to his island, to spread his country's influence on the world's stage and keep his islanders safe and prosperous.

As he neared the children, with his courtiers keeping a discreet distance, their small faces turned to him with curiosity. As often happened, it took only one to recognise him before his identity spread like wildfire and they all came running up. It was one of the things he so liked about children: their lack of inhibition. In a world of politeness and protocol he found it refreshing.

One thing he and Catalina were in agreement about was the wish for a minimum of two children. They agreed on many things. Most things. Which was a good omen for their forthcoming marriage. On paper, everything about their union appeared perfect. But...

Every time he tried to picture the children they would create together his mind came up blank. The picture just would not form.

Despite her ravishing beauty, his blood had yet to thicken for her. But this was only a minor issue, and one he was certain would resolve itself the more time he spent with her. Tomorrow he would fly to Monte Cleure so he could formally ask her father for Catalina's hand in marriage. It was only a formality, but one that couldn't be overlooked.

At least times had moved on from such issues as a dowry having to be found and trade alliances and so on being written into the contract of any royal betrothal. Now all he had to worry about was his bride having blue blood.

He'd always found blue so cold.

He turned his attention on the English children and answered a host of questions from them, including, 'Is it true your toilet is made of gold?'

His personal favourite was 'Is it true you carry a sub-machine gun wherever you go?'

In answer to this he pulled from his pocket the penknife his grandfather had given him on his graduation from Sandhurst; an upgraded version of the one he'd been given on his tenth birthday. 'No, but I always carry *this*.'

As expected, the children were agog to see

it. It was termed a penknife only in the loosest sense; on sight anyone would recognise it for the deadly fighting instrument it truly was. Children loved it when he showed it to them. Their basic human nature had not yet been knocked out of them by the insane political correctness infecting the rest of the Western world.

'Most Agonites carry knives with them,' he said to the enthralled children. 'If anyone wants to invade our island they know we will fight back with force.'

Their teacher, who had looked at the knife as if it had come personally from Eurynomos himself, looked most relieved as she glanced at her watch. Immediately she clapped her hands together. 'Everyone into their pairs—it's time for our tour.'

Today was Thursday…Amy was taking on some of the tours…

The hairs on the back of his neck lifted. He looked over at the museum entrance. A slender figure stood at the top of the steps. Even though she was too far away for him to see clearly, the increasing beat of his heart told him it was her.

He straightened, a smile playing on his lips.

Only two days had passed since she'd called his bluff and walked out of the boardroom, leaving him with an ache in his groin he'd only just recovered from. He would bet anything she had suffered in the same manner. He would bet she'd spent the past two days jumping every time her phone rang, waiting for his call.

Her pride had been wounded when she'd learned he was taking a wife, but she would get over it. She couldn't punish him for ever, not when she suffered as greatly as he did. Soon she would come crawling back.

After a moment's thought, he beckoned for one of his courtiers and instructed him to pass his apologies to his brothers. They could handle the meeting without him.

The time was ripe to assist Amy in crawling back to him.

The Agon palace dungeons never failed to thrill, whatever the visitor's age. Set deep underground, and reached by steep winding staircases at each end of the gloom, only those over the age of eight were permitted to enter. Inside, dim light was provided by tiny electrical candles that flickered as if they were the real thing, casting shadows wherever one stood. Unsurprisingly, the children today were huddled closely together.

'These dungeons were originally a pit in which to throw the Venetian invaders,' Amy said, speaking clearly so all twenty-three children on the tour could hear. 'The Venetians were the only people to successfully invade Agon, and when Ares the Conqueror, cousin of the King at the time, led the uprising in AD 1205, the first thing he ordered his men to do was build these pits. King Timios, who was the reigning King and whom the Agonites blamed for letting the Venetians in, was thrown into the cell to my left.'

The children took it in turns to gawp through the iron railings at the tiny square stone pit.

'The manacle on the right-hand wall is the original manacle used to chain him,' she added.

'Did he die in here?' a young boy asked.

'No,' said a deep male voice that reverberated off the narrow walls before she could answer, making them all jump.

A long shadow cast over them and Helios appeared. In the flickering light of the damp passageway in which they stood his large frame appeared magnified, as if Orion, the famously handsome giant, had come to life.

What was he *doing* here?

She'd seen him only an hour ago, standing in the gardens talking to the school parties, as at ease with the children as he was in every other situation. That had been the moment she had forgotten how to breathe.

It will get better, she kept assuring herself. *It's still early days and still raw. Soon you'll feel better.*

'King Timios was held in these cells for six months before Ares Patakis expelled him and, with the consent of the people, took the crown for himself,' Helios said to the captivated children. 'The palace was built over these dungeons so King Ares could have personal control over the prisoners.'

'Did he kill anyone?' asked the same bloodthirsty boy.

'He killed many people,' Helios answered solemnly. 'But only in battle. Prisoners of war were released and sent back to Venice.' He paused and offered a smile. 'But only after having their hands chopped off. King Ares wanted to send a warning to other armies wishing to invade—*Step on our shores and you will never wield a weapon again.* That's if they were lucky enough to live.'

The deeper they went into the dungeons, which were large enough to hold up to three hundred prisoners, the more questions were thrown at him as the children did their best to spook each other in the candlelit dimness.

It was with relief that Helios handled everything asked of him—his presence had made her tongue tie itself into a knot.

'Have *you* ever killed anyone?' an undersized girl asked with a nervous laugh.

He shook his head slowly. 'But since I could walk and talk I've been trained to use knives, shoot arrows and throw a spear. My brothers and I are all military trained. Trust me, should any other nation try to invade us, Agonites are ready. We fight. We are not afraid to spill blood—whether it's an enemy's or our own—to protect what's ours. We will defend our island to the death.'

Utter silence followed this impassioned speech. Twenty-three sets of wide eyes gazed up at Helios with a mixture of awe and terror. The teacher looked shell-shocked.

It had had the opposite effect on Amy.

His words had pushed through her skin to heat her veins. It had never so much been his looks, as gorgeous as he was, that had attracted her. It had been his passion. The Kalliakis family was a dynasty whose blood ran red, not blue. And no one's blood ran redder than Helios's. On the outside he was a true prince. Beneath his skin lay a warrior.

'And that, children, proves that it's not only Ares the Conqueror's blood Prince Helios has inherited from his ancestor but his devotion to his homeland.' Amy spoke quickly, to break the hush and to distract herself from the ache spreading inside her. 'Now, who here would like to be adopted by the Prince? Any takers? No? Hmm… You surprise me. Come on, then, who wants to visit the museum gift shop?'

That brought them back to life; the thought of spending their money on gifts for themselves.

'It's a good thing you'll never have to be a tour

guide as your day job,' Amy couldn't resist saying to Helios as she climbed the stairs a little way behind the school party. 'They'll all have nightmares.'

He followed closely behind her. 'They're learning my family's history. I was putting it into the context of the present day for them.'

'Yes. They were learning about your *history*. There's a big difference between hearing about wars and blood-spilling from centuries ago and having it put into the here and now, especially in the dungeons, of all places. They're only ten years old.'

'The world is full of bloodshed. That's never changed in the history of mankind. The only way to stop it creeping to our shores is through fear and stability.'

Her hand tightened on the railing as she carried on climbing. 'But Agon *is* stable. You have an elected senate. You are a democracy.'

'The people still look to us, their royal family, for leadership. Our opinions matter. Our actions matter even more so.'

'Hence the reason you're marrying Princess Catalina,' she stated flatly.

'We are a prosperous, stable island nation, *matakia mou*, and it's the hard work of generations of my family that has made it so. Until the entire world is stable we are vulnerable to attack in many different forms. We lead by example, and as a people we are united as one. Stability within the royal family promotes stability for the whole island. My grandfather is dying. My marriage will bring peace to him and act as security to my people, who will be assured that the future of my family is taken care of and by extension their own families too. They know that with a descendant of Ares Patakis on the throne their country is not only ready to defend itself but able to weather any financial storm that may hit our isles.'

Somewhere during his speech they'd both stopped climbing. Amy found herself facing him from two steps above, coming to eye level with him. His eyes were liquid, the shadows dancing over his features highlighting the strength of the angles and planes that made him so darkly handsome. Her fingers tingled with the urge to reach out and touch him...

'I need to catch up with the children,' she

breathed, but her rubbery legs made no attempt to move.

'They know where they're going,' he murmured, placing a hand on the damp wall to steady himself as he leaned in close.

His other hand caught her hip, jerking her to him. Delicious heat swirled through her; moisture pushed out the dryness in her mouth. Her skin danced and her lips parted as she moved her mouth to meet his…

She only just pulled away in time.

Swiping at his hand to remove it from her hip, she said, 'I haven't said goodbye to them.'

'Then say your goodbyes.' His eyes were alight with amusement. 'Keep running, *matakia mou*, but know you can't run for ever. Soon I will catch you.'

She didn't answer, turning tail and racing to the top of the steep staircase, gripping tightly onto the rail, and then out into the corridor.

At least in the corridor she could breathe.

What had just happened? She'd been a breath away from kissing him. Did she have no pride? No sense of preservation?

She wanted to cry with frustration.

Whether Helios believed it or not, they were over. He was marrying someone else. It was abhorrent that she still reacted so strongly towards him.

There was only one thing she could do.

She had to leave.

As soon as the exhibition was officially opened, to coincide with the Gala in just over a fortnight, she would leave the palace and never come back.

After a long day spent overseeing the arrival of artefacts from the Greek museum Amy should have been dead on her feet, but the email she'd just received had acted like a shot of espresso to her brain.

After months of searching and weeks of tentative communication, Leander had agreed to see her. Tomorrow night she would meet her half-brother for the first time.

She looked at her watch. If she moved quickly she could run to Resina and buy herself a new dress to wear for their meal, before late-night shopping was over. She wouldn't have time to-

morrow, with Saturday being the museum's busiest day.

After hurriedly turning her computer off and
shuffling papers so her desk looked tidy, and
not as if she'd abandoned it whilst in the middle
of important work, she rushed out of her office
and headed downstairs to see if Pedro was still
about and could lock up.

She came to an abrupt halt.

There, in the museum entrance, talking to
Pedro, stood Helios.

She wasn't quick enough to escape. Both of
them turned their faces to her.

'Speak of the woman and she shall appear,'
said Pedro, beaming at her.

'What have I done?' she asked, squashing the
butterflies in her stomach and feigning nonchalance.

Pedro grinned. 'Don't look so worried. Helios
and I have been discussing your future.'

Within the confines of the museum the staff
addressed Helios by his first name, at his insis-
tence.

'Oh?' Her gaze fell on Helios. 'I thought you

were going to Monte Cleure,' she said before she could stop herself.

'My plane leaves in an hour.'

Her chest compressed in on itself. Stupidly, she'd looked up the distance between Agon and Monte Cleure, which came in at just over one thousand two hundred miles. Just over two and a half hours' flying time. With the time difference factored in he would be there in time to share an intimate dinner with the Princess.

She pressed her lips together to prevent the yelp of pain that wanted to escape and forced her features into an expression of neutrality. Helios had so much power over her she couldn't bear for him to know how deeply it ran.

Oblivious to any subtext going on around him, Pedro said, 'I was going to leave this until tomorrow, but seeing as you're here there's no time like the present—'

'We were saying how impressed we are with your handling of the exhibition,' Helios cut in smoothly. 'You have exceeded our expectations. We would like to offer you a permanent job at the museum when your secondment finishes.'

'What kind of job?' she asked warily. A week

ago this news would have filled her with joy. But everything was different now.

'Corinna will be leaving us at the end of the summer. We would like you to have her job.'

Corinna was second only to Pedro in the museum hierarchy.

'There are far more qualified curators than me working here,' she said non-committally, wishing Pegasus might fly into the palace at that very moment and whisk her away to safety.

'Pedro is happy to train you in the areas where you lack experience,' said Helios, a smile of triumph dancing in his eyes. 'The important thing is you can do the job. Everyone here likes and respects you...curators at other museums enjoy collaborating with you. You're an asset to the Agon Palace Museum and we would be fools to let you go.'

If Pedro hadn't been there she would have cursed Helios for such a blatant act of manipulation.

'What do you think?' he asked when she remained silent. His dark eyes bored into her, a knowing, almost playful look emanating from them. 'How do you like the idea of living and working here permanently?'

She knew exactly what he was doing and exactly what he was thinking. He knew how much she loved her job, his island and its people. Helios was working tactically. He thought that if he threw enough incentives at her she would be so overcome with gratitude she would allow him back into her bed.

She'd entered their relationship without any illusions of permanency. It had suited her as much as it had suited him. Desire was what had glued them together, and it scared her to know that despite all the protective barriers she'd placed around herself he'd still slipped inside. Not fully, but enough for pain to lance her whenever she thought of him and the Princess together. When she thought of her own future without him in her life.

How could she continue to be his lover feeling as she did now, even putting aside the fact of his imminent engagement?

His engagement had hammered home as nothing else could that she was good enough to share his bed but not good enough for anything more.

She knew she was being unfair—Agon's constitution and Helios's position in life were not his fault or within his control—but for the first time she felt the reality on an emotional level and that terrified her.

In her heart of hearts she'd always longed to meet someone she could trust with the truth about her conception and not fear they would turn away in disgust or believe that the fruit never fell far from the tree. To meet someone who could love her for herself.

During their time together she had come to trust Helios. He was a man she'd thought she could confide the truth to, and she was almost certain he wouldn't turn away in disgust. But still she'd kept her secrets close. He couldn't give her the other things she'd always secretly craved but had never quite believed she deserved. Love. Fidelity. Commitment. It had been wiser to keep her heart as close as her secrets.

She considered her words carefully, although her head swam. 'I'm going to need time to think about it.'

'What is there to think about?' he asked, his dark eyes narrowing slightly.

'My life is in England,' she said evenly, although she knew there was really nothing to think about. He could offer to quadruple her salary and the answer would be the same.

She was saved from elaborating by Helios's phone ringing.

'My cue to leave,' he said, flashing her a grin. 'We can continue this discussion another time soon.'

She knew what 'soon' meant. He meant to visit her on Sunday evening, when he returned.

With Pedro there she was in no position to refuse or challenge anything. And even if she'd wanted to Helios didn't give her the chance, wishing them both a good weekend before striding off and out of the museum. On his way to Monte Cleure to spend his weekend with the Princess and her family.

And she…

As soon as she returned from her last-minute shopping trip she would write her resignation letter. She would give it to Pedro tomorrow, safe in the knowledge that Helios would be over a thousand miles away.

CHAPTER FOUR

AMY PUT THE lip gloss tube to her mouth, but before she could squeeze the gel-like substance on, a loud rap made her jerk her hand back. The banging had come from the door outside her bedroom that connected the passageway between her apartment and Helios's.

She pressed her hand to her pounding heart.

What was he doing here?

He was supposed to be spending the whole weekend in Monte Cleure, using his time there to officially ask Princess Catalina's father's blessing for their marriage. He should still be there, celebrating their forthcoming union, not here on Agon, banging on his ex-lover's door.

Breathing heavily, she closed her eyes and willed him away.

Another loud rap on the door proved the futility of her wish.

Suddenly galvanised into action, she dropped

the lip gloss into her handbag and slipped out of her room, hurrying past the connecting door as another knock rang out. Snatching her jacket off the coat stand, she left her apartment through the main exit and hurried down the narrow stairs. With her heart battering against her chest she punched in the code that opened the door and stole outside into the warm spring evening air.

She felt like an escaped convict.

Security lights blazed everywhere, and she kept as close to the palace wall as she could for as long as she could until she had to dart out to cross into the courtyard used by the palace staff. The car she'd ordered earlier was already waiting for her. She jumped straight into the passenger side, making Eustachys the driver, who was busy on his phone, jump.

'You're early,' he said with a grin, before adding, 'Where do you want to go?'

She forced a smile. Whenever she needed one of the pool of cars and drivers that were on permanent standby for the palace staff she was invariably given Eustachys, who spoke excellent English. 'Resina, please.'

She gave him the name of the restaurant she

was dining at and tried not to betray her impatience as he inputted it into his satnav, especially as she was perfectly aware that he knew every inch of the island and had no need for it.

A minute later they were off, starting the twenty-minute drive to Agon's capital, a cosmopolitan town rich in history and full of excellent shops and restaurants.

She didn't want to think of Helios, still standing at her door demanding entry. She didn't want to think of him at all.

All she wanted at that moment was to keep her composure as she met the man who shared her blood for the first time.

When Eustachys collected her from the restaurant later that evening Resina's streets were full of Saturday night revellers and stars were twinkling down from the black sky above them.

Amy's head throbbed too hard for her to want to be out amongst them.

Although not a complete disaster, her meeting with Leander had been much more difficult than she'd anticipated. It hadn't helped that she'd still been shaken from Helios's unexpected return to Agon and that she'd been half expecting him to turn up at the restaurant. Discovering where she'd gone would have been as easy for him as buttoning a shirt.

Leander hadn't helped either. She'd already gathered from his social media profile and his posts that he wasn't the most mature of men, but now, reflecting on their meal together—which she had paid for with no argument from him—she came to the sad conclusion that her newly found half-brother was a spoilt brat.

He'd been honest as far as he'd wanted to be. He'd told his mother—Amy's birth mother—about their meeting. He'd made it clear to Amy that it would be his judgement alone that would determine whether Neysa would meet the child she'd abandoned, and that power was a wonderful thing for him to crow about.

Scrap being a spoilt brat. Her half-brother was a monster.

Through all the crowing and the sniffing—she was almost certain he was on drugs—Amy had gleaned that his wealthy father had no idea of her existence. The Soukises had a nice, cosy life, and Amy turning up was in none of their interests. As far as Leander was concerned, Amy was a can of worms that was one twist of the can opener away from potentially destroying his comfortable life.

So, their meeting hadn't been a *complete* Greek tragedy. But not far off.

After being dropped back in the courtyard she made her way on weary legs to her apartment, removing her heels to walk up the staircase to her apartment.

She couldn't elicit the tiniest bit of surprise at finding Helios on her sofa, feet bare, in snug-fitting faded jeans and a black T-shirt, his muscular arms folded in a manner she knew meant only one thing—trouble.

'How did you get in here?' she asked pointlessly. This was his palace. He could go where he pleased.

'With a key,' he answered sardonically, straightening up and rolling his shoulders. 'Where have you been?'

'Out.'

Helios threw her a stare with narrowed eyes, taking in the pretty mint-green dress that fell to her knees, the elegantly knotted hair and the hooped earrings. It was an outfit he'd never seen her wear before. 'Have you been on a date?'

She gazed at him with tired eyes. 'It doesn't matter where I've been. Shouldn't you be with your fiancée? I assume she *is* your fiancée now?'

'Her father gave his blessing. We will make the official announcement during the Gala.'

'So why aren't you in Monte Cleure, celebrating?'

'Some unwelcome news was brought to my attention, so I came back a day early.'

A flicker of alarm flashed across her pretty features. 'Has something happened to your grandfather?'

'My grandfather's fine.' As fine as an eighty-seven-year-old man riddled with cancer could be.

He visited his grandfather every day that he was in the country, always praying that a miracle had occurred and he would see signs of improvement. All he ever saw was further deterioration. The strong, vibrant man who'd been not just the head of his family but the very heart of it was diminishing before his eyes.

Helios and his brothers' business interests had been so successful that their islanders no longer had to pay a cent of tax towards the royal family's upkeep and security. They had enough money to keep their people afloat if the worst economic storm should hit. But not even their great wealth was enough to cure the man who had given up so much to raise them, and it hadn't been enough to cure their beloved grandmother of the pneumonia that had killed her five years ago either. Her death was something their grandfather had never recovered from.

But for once, this evening, he had hardly thought of his grandfather. He'd been sitting rigidly on Amy's hard sofa, trying to keep a lid on his temper as the hours had passed and he'd waited for her to return.

And now here she was, dressed for a romantic night out *with someone else*. It was the final punch in the guts after what had been a hellish day.

The straightforward task of asking the King of Monte Cleure for his daughter's hand in marriage had turned into something infinitely more stomach-turning. The King had received him as if he were a long-lost son, his pride and happiness in his daughter's choice and her future prospects evident.

Throughout the entire private audience a bad taste had been lodged in Helios's throat. Words had formed but he'd spoken them as if they were being dragged over spikes. And throughout all the formalities his brain had been ticking over Amy's less than enthusiastic response to his offer of a permanent role at the palace museum.

To Helios it had been the perfect solution—a way to prove to Amy that she still had a role to play in his life for as long as she wanted, and that he wasn't throwing away what they had for the sake of a piece of paper tying him to another woman. And, besides, she'd earned the job offer. All his reasoning, everything he'd said to her, had been the truth.

Her response had grated on him.

And then he'd received that message from Pedro and taken his jet straight back to Agon.

'Where have you been?' he asked for a second time, noting the way she avoided his gaze at the question.

She sank onto the armchair in the corner, put a palm to her eye and rubbed it, smearing a trail of smoky-grey make-up across her cheek. 'You have no right to ask. Who I see and what I do with my time is my own business.'

'If you have taken another lover then I have every right to question you about it,' he retorted, smothering the nausea roiling in his guts. If she'd taken another lover…

'No, you *don't*,' she said hotly. 'You're the one marrying someone else, not me. That makes me a free agent. I don't owe you anything.'

Staring at her angry face, it struck him for the first time that Amy was serious about their relationship being over. Until that precise moment he'd assumed her pride and jealousy had been speaking for her. That she'd been punishing him.

'Who have you been with?' he demanded. 'Was it a man?'

She met his eyes and gave a sharp nod.

'Is it someone I know?'

'No.'

'Where did you meet him?'

'That doesn't matter.' She sucked in a breath. 'Look, Helios—please—leave me alone. What we had…it's over…'

'So you've jumped straight into bed with another man? Is this your way of punishing me for doing my duty to my family and my country?'

The distaste that flashed over her face answered for her. 'That's disgusting.'

He hid the immediate rush of relief that she hadn't been intimate with this elusive man. The relief died as quickly as it had been born.

'If you're not punishing me then why were you out with someone else? Are you so keen to prove your point that we're finished that you'd humiliate me?'

'How is me dining with someone else humiliating? And how can you dare say that when you're the one *marrying* someone else?'

'And how can *you* dare think I'll let you walk away?'

She stilled, her eyes widening, the flicker under her left eye returning.

'The reason I came back early from Monte Cleure is because Pedro called to inform me that the curator in charge of my grandfather's Jubilee Exhibition—a woman who, may I remind you, was taken on despite her lack of experience, because Pedro and I were both convinced she had the knowledge and enthusiasm to pull it off—has decided to quit five months early.'

His anger burned, enflaming him. He would never have believed Amy could be so underhand.

'Helios…' She reached out a hand, then dropped it back to her side with a sigh. 'What other choice do I have? I can't stay here now.'

'You're not the heroine of some old-fashioned melodrama,' he said scathingly. 'What did you think would happen? That I would hear you had resigned and shrug my shoulders and say that it's okay? Or that I would be so upset at the thought of you leaving my life permanently I would abandon my plans to marry Catalina, re-nounce my claim to the throne and marry you?'

She clutched at the knot of hair at the nape of her neck. 'I hoped you would accept it and at least try to understand where I'm coming from.'

'Well I don't understand or accept it. Your res-ignation has been refused. You will stay until your contracted period is up or I will sue you for breach of contract.'

Her shock was visible. 'You wouldn't…'

'Wouldn't I? Leave before September and see for yourself.'

'The exhibition is almost complete,' she said, breathing heavily, angry colour heightening her cheeks. 'Come the Gala and we'll be ready for visitors—my job will be done. Anyone else can carry on.'

'"Anyone else" will not have the breadth of knowledge you've developed about my grandfather and our ancestors. You signed that contract and you will damn well fulfil it.'

She jumped to her feet, her hands balled into fists. 'Why are you doing this? Why can't you just let me go?'

'Because we belong together,' he snarled. 'You're mine—do you understand that?'

'No, the *Princess* belongs to you. Not me. I belong only to myself. You can insist I work the rest of my contract—that's absolutely within your rights—but that doesn't change anything else. I will work out the contract if I must, but I will not share your bed. I will not be your mistress.'

Helios could feel the blood pumping in his head. His veins were aflame; needles were pushing into his skin. Deep in his gut was something he couldn't identify—but, *Theos*, whatever it was, it hurt.

He'd known from the outset that Amy was a woman of honour. Her excitement at his job offer had been so evident it had been contagious, but she'd refused to agree or to sign the contract until she'd spoken to her bosses at the British Museum face-to-face. If there had been any hesitation from them in letting her take the role she would have refused it, even though it was, by her own admission, a dream come true.

If it was such a dream then why was she prepared to walk away from it now?

And if she was so honourable how could she already be actively seeking a new lover?

He needed to get out of this apartment before he did something he would regret. So many emotions were riding through him it was impossible to distinguish them. He only knew his fists wanted nothing more than to smash things, to take every ornament and piece of furniture in this apartment and pulverise it.

For the second time in as many weeks the violence that lived in his blood threatened to boil over, and he despised himself for it almost as much as he despised Amy right now for seeking to leave him. But, unlike his violent father, Helios knew his own temper would never be di-

MICHELLE SMART   89

rected at a woman. It was the only certainty he could take comfort from.

Striding over to her, he took her chin in his hand and forced her to look at him. *Theos*, she had such delicate features and such gorgeous skin. He didn't think there was an inch of her he hadn't stroked and kissed. He refused to believe he would never make love to her again. He *refused*.

'If you understand nothing else, understand this—you will *always* belong to me,' he said roughly, before dropping his hold and walking out of her apartment.

Amy's phone vibrated, breaking her concentration on the beautiful green sapphire ring she was supposed to be categorising but instead could only stare at with a lump in her throat.

This ring had belonged to Helios's mother. This ring would one day soon slide onto Princess Catalina's finger.

The message from Leander was simple and clear.

She doesn't want to meet you. Do not contact me again.

She read it a number of times before closing her eyes and rubbing at the nape of her neck. A burn stung the back of her retinas.

She had never expected her birth mother to welcome her long-abandoned daughter with cheers and whistles, but she had expected *something*. Some curiosity, if nothing else. Did she not even wonder what Amy looked like? Or who she had become?

But there was too much shame. To Neysa Soukis, Amy was nothing but a scar on her memories; a scar that had to remain hidden.

If Amy were a different person she would force the issue. She would stalk Neysa at her house until she was browbeaten into seeing her. But even if she was capable of doing that what would it accomplish? Nothing more than Neysa's further contempt and probably a restraining order to boot.

All she wanted was to talk to her. Just once. But clearly she wasn't worth even that.

'Are you ready to go yet?'

Blinking rapidly, she looked up and found Greta standing in the doorway.

Amy turned her phone off. 'She doesn't want to meet me.'

At least with Greta she didn't have to pretend.

Greta came over to her and put an arm around her back. 'I'm sorry.'

Amy sniffed. 'I just thought…'

'I know,' said Greta softly. 'But learning you were here probably came as a big shock to her. She'll change her mind.'

'What if she doesn't?'

'She will,' Greta insisted. 'Now, turn your computer off. We've a night out to get ready for.'

'I'm not going.'

'You are. A night out is exactly what you need.'

'But Helios will be there.'

'So what? This will be your chance to let him see you having a great time and that you're completely unaffected by your break-up.'

Amy gave a laugh that came out as more of a snort than anything else. Thank God for Greta. Without her cheering friendship and positive attitude life on Agon would be unbearable right now.

Was it only four months ago that she'd arrived on this island full of excitement for what the future held? With a handsome prince as her boss and the opportunity to find the woman who'd given birth to her?

Now she was stuck here for another five months, and she would have to watch the handsome prince marry his princess and her birth mother wanted nothing to do with her.

She wished she'd never come to Agon.

Greta rubbed her arm in solidarity. 'Let's get your dress and go back to my flat. There's a bottle of ouzo waiting for us.'

'But…'

'Are you going to give that man so much power over you that you'd give up a free night out with all your friends and colleagues?'

Amy sighed and shook her head. Greta was right. She'd spent the past four days hiding away, mostly holing herself up in the museum's enormous basement, on the pretext of categorising artefacts, desperate to avoid bumping into Helios. And she'd been successful—other than one brief glimpse of him in the palace gardens she'd not had any dealings with him. Of course he was incredibly busy, with the Gala being only ten days away.

'Maybe he won't come,' she said with sudden hopefulness.

'Maybe...' Greta didn't look convinced.

But the thought of him not coming made her feel just as rotten as the thought of him being there.

If he did come, she had to pray he didn't bring the Princess as his guest.

To meet his future wife in the flesh would be one wound too many.

CHAPTER FIVE

THE MAIN REASON Helios had chosen Hotel Giroud for the staff night out was because his staff deserved to enjoy themselves in the most exclusive hotel on Agon. The fact its gardens led to a private beach was a plus.

Owned by Nathaniel Giroud, an old friend from his schooldays, it was the sister establishment of Club Giroud, the most exclusive and secret club on the island. The hotel was only marginally more inclusive, provided one had the funds and the connections. The quality of Helios's connections went without saying, and of course he had the funds, more than he could ever spend. He didn't begrudge spending a cent of his money on the staff who worked so hard for him.

He took his museum staff out twice a year: once at the beginning of the summer season, and once right at the end. Although the events weren't compulsory everyone attended, even those curators and conservators who would live in the museum basement if he'd let them. Most of his museum staff were a breed unto themselves, deeply dedicated to their work. He'd never imagined he would *desire* one of them.

And yet he had. He did.

During what was possibly the busiest time of his life, he couldn't flush Amy from his mind. Even after the news his brother Theseus had given him a couple of days ago he couldn't rid himself of her. Here he was, wrestling with the bombshell that Theseus had a secret child, a Kalliakis heir, and still she remained at the forefront of his mind.

It was taking everything he had to keep away from the museum. There was far too much going on for him to spend any time there, but knowing Amy was within its spacious walls meant the place acted like a magnet to him.

There were only ten days now until the Gala, and he had a mountain of work to do for it. He was determined to make it a success for his grandfather and for all his people.

On Agon, heirs traditionally took the throne at the age of forty. His father had died a few years short of that age and so his grandfather—without a word of complaint—had abandoned his retirement plans to hold the throne for Helios. His grandparents had sacrificed their dreams of travelling the world and his grandmother had put aside her thoughts of returning to her first love of performing as violin virtuoso. Those dreams had been abandoned so they could raise their orphaned grandchildren and mould them into princes the whole of Agon could be proud of. They had sacrificed everything.

There was no person on this earth Helios respected more or felt a deeper affection for than his grandfather. He would do anything for him. And, out of everything, it was marriage he knew his grandfather wanted the most for him. King Astraeus the Fourth wanted to leave this world secure in the knowledge that his lineage would live on and that the monarchy was in safe hands.

Although his engagement was now an open secret, the official announcement would bring his grandfather peace. That more than anything was Helios's overriding concern. He didn't like to think what it would bring for his own state of mind.

Catalina wouldn't return to Agon until the Gala. He'd dissuaded her from coming any earlier, using his busyness as an excuse to keep her away. A shudder ran through him as he recalled her obvious disappointment when he'd left Monte Cleure a day early. When he'd said goodbye she'd raised her chin in anticipation of his kiss. The most he'd been able to do was brush his lips against her cheek. She'd smelled fantastic, and she'd looked beautiful, but he might as well have been dead from the waist down for all she did for him.

Catalina knew what she was marrying into, he reminded himself. She had no illusions that their union would ever be about love. She'd assured him of that herself. But now he wondered if mutual respect would be enough when he couldn't even bring himself to kiss her.

He stood in the hotel lobby, personally greeting his staff and their partners. In all, over one hundred people were expected. He always enjoyed seeing their transformation, enjoyed seeing the back-room staff, who tended to live in jeans and baggy tops, and the front-line staff, who wore smart uniforms, all dressed to the nines in smart suits and cocktail dresses.

As each person entered he welcomed them with an embrace while Talia, his private secretary, handed them all an envelope.

Soon the lobby was full and waiting staff with trays of champagne were circulating. Conversation was stilted, as it always was at the beginning of such evenings, but he knew that wouldn't last long. Once everyone had had a drink or two their inhibitions would fall away and they would enjoy themselves properly. They all worked so hard they deserved to let their hair down.

Through the lobby's wide glass doors he saw two figures approach, their heads bent close together, laughing. His heart jolted, making him lose the thread of the conversation he'd struck up with one of the tour guides. Closer they came, until they reached the doors and showed their identification to the guards on duty, who inspected them closely before standing to one side to admit them.

The doors opened automatically and in they walked.

He greeted Greta first, with the same kind of

embrace he'd shared with everyone else. She returned it warmly, gushing about how excited she was. And then it was time to greet Amy.

The same smile she'd entered the lobby with stayed fixed on her face, but her eyes told a different story.

His throat ran dry.

He'd seen her dressed up on a few occasions before: when he'd taken her out on dates away from the palace, and last weekend for her 'date' with someone else, but tonight…

Theos. She looked stunning.

She wore a sleeveless navy blue chiffon dress that floated just above her knees, with silver diamond-shaped beads layered along the hem and across the high round neckline. On her feet were simple high-heeled black shoes that showcased her slender legs. She'd left her dark blonde hair loose, so that it fell across her shoulders and down her back. Her large taupe eyes were ringed with dark grey eyeshadow and her delectable lips were painted nude.

He couldn't drag his eyes away.

For what had to be the first time ever he found himself at a loss for words.

Judging by the expression in her wide eyes, pain emanating from them as she gazed back at him, she was struggling to form words on her own tongue too.

It was Greta who broke the silence, with a shout of, 'Champagne!' She grinned at Helios, slipped her arm through Amy's and whisked her off to find them a glass each.

'Thanks,' Amy muttered the second they were out of his earshot. Her heart was hammering so hard she could swear she was suffering from palpitations.

'You're welcome. Here,' said Greta, thrusting a glass into Amy's hand. 'Drink this.'

'I've had enough already.' They'd had a couple of shots of ouzo each in Greta's flat, before the car had arrived for them, and while not drunk she definitely felt a little light-headed.

Greta shook her head. 'You're going to need a lot more than this to get through the night without throwing yourself at him.'

'I'm not going to throw myself at him.'

'You could have fooled me from the way you were just staring at each other.'

'We're over,' Amy stated flatly.

'So you keep telling yourself.'

'I mean it.'

'I know you do. The problem is I don't think your heart believes it.' Greta squeezed her hand. 'Don't worry. I'll stop you from entering the big bad wolf's clutches again.'

Fighting to stop her gaze flickering back to him, Amy nodded and swallowed half of her champagne.

'Let's see what's in these envelopes,' Greta said, ripping hers open.

Amy followed suit and found inside a personalised card, thanking her for all her hard work since joining the museum, and two hundred euros to spend in the casino.

'Last year we spent a day on Helios's yacht,' Greta confided, fingering her own pile of notes lovingly. 'It was amazing—when we got back to shore Talia was so drunk Pedro had to carry her off.'

Her words did the trick, making Amy laugh at the image of Helios's prim private secretary, brought along to keep events ticking along smoothly, losing control of herself in such a manner.

Some of her angst loosened and she made a pledge to enjoy herself. At some point just about *everyone* who'd had a work-based affair had to deal with an ex being present. She didn't have to make a big deal of it. If she stuck to Greta's side and avoided even looking at Helios she would be fine.

But stopping herself from staring became harder when they were taken through to the restaurant, which had been put aside for their private use. The seating plan meant she had an excellent view of the top table, where Helios was seated. So good was her view that the moment she took her seat his eyes found her.

She cast her eyes down to her menu, ostensibly familiarising herself with her selections. When she dared to look back up he was engaged in conversation with Jessica, an American curator who had worked at the museum for two decades.

'You're staring,' Greta hissed.

Smiling tightly, Amy forced small talk from her lips, taking a small breath of relief when the starters were brought out.

Her plate was placed before her, and the waiter removed the silver lid with a flourish to release the beautiful aromas of roast sea scallops and smoked celeriac purée sitting in a shellfish broth. It tasted as wonderful as it smelled, and she wished she could appreciate it more, but as hard as she tried her awareness of Helios two tables away was all-consuming.

She was powerless to stop her eyes flickering to him, taking in the strong brown throat exposed by his unbuttoned white silk shirt—all the other men wore ties—and the way his dark blue dinner jacket emphasised the breadth of his chest. If she could only ever stare at one thing for the rest of her life it would be him.

He was laughing at something Jessica had said, his generous smile wide, his liquid eyes lively. A burst of jealousy ripped through her to see him enjoying Jessica's company so much, a totally irrational feeling, considering that Jessica was old enough to be his mother, but real nonetheless.

It was some consolation that he hadn't brought the Princess with him. If she'd had to watch him talking and laughing with her, Amy was certain she would have been sick.

And then his gaze found hers again and her

stomach somersaulted. He raised his glass of wine slowly and took a long swallow.

An elbow in her ribs brought her back to earth.

'Stop it!' Greta whispered fiercely.

But she couldn't.

Even when her main course of fillet of beef and truffle mash was brought out to her she couldn't stop her eyes from constantly darting to him.

There was nothing wrong in looking, she told herself helplessly. So long as she kept away from him she could look. She just couldn't touch.

After what felt like hours the meal was over. Before she could flee into the casino, away from the magnetism of Helios's stare, he was on his feet and making a speech, which ended with him raising his glass and offering a toast to them all.

'If you'd all make your way to the private beach at midnight you'll find a last surprise for you,' he finished with a grin. 'Until then, enjoy the casino and the music and most of all have fun—you've earned it.'

Keeping herself glued to Greta's side, Amy headed into the casino, which was every bit as opulent as she'd expected and very busy. However, Helios had arranged for them to have their own private poker, blackjack and roulette tables. She had no interest in playing but it was fun to observe, especially to watch Jessica, who seemed to be cleaning up on the blackjack table, to everyone's amazement. There was soon a crowd forming around her.

The only blot on the landscape was a prickle on her neck: the weight of Helios's stare upon her. It took everything she had not to return it. Without the dining tables separating them she felt vulnerable. It was only a matter of time before he sought her out.

Except it never happened. From out of the corner of her eye she watched him make his way around the casino and the adjoining dance room, speaking to all his staff in turn, his easy smile evident.

So many free drinks were being pressed into their hands that Amy felt herself becoming more light-headed by the minute. Soon it was enough to make herself switch to coffee.

She couldn't stop her heart from jolting every time Helios moved away from one person and on to another. Irrationally, she longed for him to bestow his attentions on her. But other than with his eyes he made no such attempt. She must be the only member of staff he hadn't made an effort to speak to. Apart from Greta, who hadn't let Amy out of her sight all evening.

Maybe he'd finally accepted that they were over, despite his proclamation that she would always be his. Maybe their short time apart had convinced him she had been right to end things between them.

A dagger speared her stomach at the thought of never feeling his strong arms around her again, or the heat of his kiss.

She needed to get out of there, to go back to her apartment and lick her wounds in peace before she gave in to the howl building in her throat. She'd done her best tonight, but not even the alcohol had numbed the ache pounding beneath her ribs. If anything, it had got worse.

But what peace could she find in her apartment when Helios was only the other side of a secret passageway? How could she survive another five months of living so close to him? With her resignation rejected and his threat of legal action if she left hanging over her head, her choices were limited. Her career would be ruined. Who would trust her if she were to breach her contract and be sued by the heir to the throne of Agon?

Because she believed that if she were to leave now he *would* carry out his threat.

He wasn't a cruel man, but when provoked Helios was hot-tempered, passionate and filled to the brim with pride. Her attempted resignation had punctured his ego.

But then, if he had finally accepted they were finished maybe he'd be more understanding and amenable to her leaving if she broached the subject again, once the Gala was over.

She wished so hard that she could hate him, but she couldn't. How could anyone hate him?

'It's nearly midnight,' Greta said animatedly. 'Let's go to the beach.'

Amy nodded. The low buzzing noise of all the surrounding chatter was making her head ache. Some fresh sea air would do her good. She'd go out and watch the last of the entertainment and then she would slip away and lick her wounds in earnest.

* * *

The hotel's curved private beach brought gasps of delight from everyone. Helios was pleased by their reaction. Indeed, the whole evening had been a marked success. He was sure there would be plenty of foggy heads in the morning, but he doubted anyone would regret them.

Rows of wooden tables with benches had been set along the sand, and gas lamps had been placed on them for illumination under the moonless sky. The hotel's beach bar was open and cocktails were being made.

To get to the beach you had to cut through the hotel's garden and follow a gentle, meandering trail, then take half a dozen steep steps down to it. It wasn't until the tables were half-full that he spotted Amy, making her way down with Greta, whom she'd clung to like a shield for the entire evening.

He knew why.

Amy didn't want to be alone because she was scared he would pounce the second he had the chance. And if she was scared of him pouncing there could only be one reason—she knew she would struggle to resist.

Her eyes had followed him everywhere that evening. She might try, but she could no more deny the chemistry between them than he could. Soon she would realise resistance was futile. Did the tide resist the pull of the moon? Of course not. Nature worked in perfect harmony, just like the desire that pulled him and Amy together.

And yet... Shadows darkened her eyes. There was pain there, the same pain he'd seen when she'd arrived at the hotel. Seeing it had made him...uneasy. It disturbed him in ways he couldn't explain, not even to himself.

It had made him think twice about approaching her. Could *he* be the cause of that pain?

When she got to the bottom of the pathway she held Greta's arm while she took her shoes off, then the pair of them took themselves to a table where some of their fellow curators were seated. Within moments of her sitting down her eyes roamed until they found him.

Even with only the soft glow of the lamps to illuminate her face he could see her yearning. He could sense her resistance waning. The uneasiness that had pulled at him all evening abated. He'd been imagining it.

With all the stress in his life—from his grandfather's deteriorating health, Theseus's shocking news, the forthcoming Gala, his own engagement and everything in between—it was no wonder his mind was playing tricks on him and making him see things that weren't there.

Music from the DJ's deck began to play; a soft dance beat for everyone to tap their bare feet to, its pulse riding through his veins.

Soon Amy would be his again. And when he got her back in his bed he was never going to let her go.

CHAPTER SIX

DESPITE HER LONGING to be away from the hotel, far from the pull of Helios, Amy was enchanted by what surrounded her. The beach, under the light of the twinkling stars, was the most perfect scene imaginable. The noise of the lapping waves mingled with the dance beat playing behind them and gave her a sense of serenity that had been missing from her life since Helios had announced his intention to marry.

'I need to use the bathroom,' Greta murmured, rising from the table. 'Are you coming?'

'I don't think you need me to hold your hand, do you?' Amy said drily.

Greta laughed and set off into the hotel on decidedly unsteady feet.

Amy shook her head with a smile. Greta had been enjoying the steady stream of free cocktails even more than Amy had enjoyed the steady stream of free coffee.

No sooner had Greta gone than two men with matching goatee beards and dreadlocks pulled back into ponytails appeared. Both were dressed in black outfits that brought to mind samurai warriors crossed with pirates. These men were Agonites; Amy would bet her savings on it.

With interpreters translating from their Greek, the two men insisted that the table Amy was seated at be moved back ten feet. As soon as that was done they drew a line in the sand, marking a semicircle which they made clear no one should cross.

Curiosity drove everyone to their feet. Without her heels on Amy had trouble seeing anything, so she ducked out of the crowd to stand at the top of the steps leading down to the beach. The extra height and distance allowed her to see unhindered.

As the men set themselves up, removing objects she couldn't see from two huge crates, Greta came out of the bathroom and made her way to the semicircle of people crowding around them.

The sun had long gone down and standing alone, without the shared body heat of the people below, Amy felt the slight chill in the air. Rubbing her arms for warmth, she kept her gaze on the men, pretending to herself that she hadn't seen Helios step out from the bar with two large cocktail glasses in his hands...

'I thought you looked thirsty,' he said, climbing the steps to stand with her.

Her heart and throat catching, she shook her head. Deep down she'd known that separating herself from the group would be perceived as an open invitation.

His smile was knowing as he handed her one of the drinks. 'Try this. I think you'll like it.'

The glass was full of crushed ice, and the liquid within it was pink. Fresh strawberries had been placed around the rim, and sprigs of mint laced the cocktail. Wordlessly, she took it from him and placed the straw between her lips.

He knew her tastes too well. 'It's delicious. What is it?'

'A strawberry mojito.'

'Did you make it?'

He laughed lightly and shook his head. 'I wouldn't know where to begin.'

She took another sip. The combination of fresh

mint and crushed strawberries played on her tongue, as did the taste of rum.

'What are you drinking?'

'A Long Island iced tea. Try some?'

She shouldn't. Really, she shouldn't.

With the moonless sky filled with twinkling stars, the scent of the sea, the background throb of music, the laughter coming from the crowd of people before them…it was a scene for romance, one she should turn and run away from.

Yet her hand disobeyed her brain, reaching out to take the glass from him, bringing the straw his own lips had wrapped around to her mouth so she could take a small sip.

Her eyes widened. 'That packs a punch!'

He grinned and took the glass back from her, brushing his fingers against hers for a second too long.

Little darts raced through her hand and up her arm. She took another sip of her mojito, fighting desperately to stop herself from leaning forward and into him. He was so close…

'I found out the other day that I'm an uncle,' Helios said, making conversation before she could remember to flee again. Besides, this was something he really needed to talk about, before his head exploded with the magnitude of it all.

'Really?'

Her shock mirrored his own initial reaction to the news. 'Theseus. He had a one-night stand with a woman he met on his sabbatical.'

'Wow. That was a few years ago, wasn't it?'

'The boy is four. His name's Toby. Theseus only found out by accident and a quirk of fate— he lied about his identity to the mother, so she was never able to tell him. And then she turned up at the palace to work on the official biography.'

'That really *is* a quirk of fate. Is he going to recognise him?'

'Yes. And he's going to marry the mother to legitimise him.'

She took another long sip of her mojito, her eyes wide as she finally met his gaze. 'Does your grandfather know?'

'Theseus is going to tell him after the Gala. We've agreed it's best to let that day be for our grandfather.'

She looked down at the ground. He wondered if she was thinking the same thing, that he was using the Gala to make the announcement of his marriage. But his announcement was different—for his grandfather it would be the pinnacle of the day, confirmation of the security that would come with knowing his heir was going to embark on matrimony.

'Theseus's relationship with my grandfather is complicated. Being a Prince of Agon is not something he's ever liked or adjusted to. It's the reason why he's been working so hard on the biography, to prove that he is ready to embrace who he is.'

'Whereas you've always embraced your destiny?' she said softly.

'I am who I am,' he answered with a shrug, not admitting that for a fleeting moment his brother's news had given him pause for thought. Theseus had a ready-made heir and a fiancée he certainly was not indifferent to…

But, no, the thought had been pushed aside before he'd allowed it to float too far into his mind. The throne would be his. It was his destiny. It was his pride. Being King was a role Theseus would hate with every fibre of his being.

Seeing Amy using her straw to fight through

the ice to the liquid left in the bottom of her glass, he signalled to a passing bartender for two more drinks.

'The news about Toby is confidential, of course,' he said, once the man had returned to the bar. 'Only you and I and Theseus's private staff know.'

'Which means half the palace knows.'

He laughed. 'The palace grapevine has a life of its own, I admit, but I hadn't heard anything before Theseus told me, so I don't think word has got out yet.'

'No one will hear anything from me.'

'That goes without saying.' In their time together he had learned to trust Amy completely. He'd never had to watch what he said to her... Apart from the time he'd failed to tell her about the real purpose behind the pre-Gala ball.

Something glistened in her eyes, a spark that flew out to touch him and cut the last of the smile from his face. Had it not been for the bartender, carrying their fresh drinks up the steps, he would have leaned in to kiss her.

Amy blinked herself out of the minor stupor

she'd been in danger of falling into and took a grateful sip of her fresh mojito.

It was crazy, but Helios's news about his nephew had brought a spark of hope within her. If there was a readymade heir in the family...

But, no. Such hopes were futile. Helios had been born to rule this great nation with a royal bride at his side. It was his destiny. And she, Amy, was a nobody.

'The entertainment's about to begin.'

'Sorry?'

That knowing smile spread once again over his handsome face. He nodded at the crowd on the beach.

Following his gaze, she saw the two piratical men standing side by side in the semicircle they'd created, their legs parted in a warrior stance. What ensued was an acrobatic display of perfect synchronicity that on its own would have been marvellous but which then switched to a whole new level.

The men ducked out of Amy's eyesight before reappearing with thick, long sticks, the ends of which were ablaze. Her mouth opened in awe as she watched them dancing and twirling and leaping and whirling whilst the fire made patterns in the darkness, bringing the very air to life.

'You look cold,' Helios murmured, stepping behind her and wrapping an arm around her waist to secure her to him.

Transfixed by what was happening on the beach, her skin dancing with something like the same flames that were playing out before her, Amy didn't resist, not even when he brought his mouth down to nuzzle into her hair. Her insides melted and despite herself she leant back into his hardness, dizzying relief rushing through her at the sensation of being back where she belonged. In Helios's arms.

She gasped as she felt his hand slide over her stomach and drift up to rest under her breasts. She knew she should throw off his hand and walk away, that allowing herself to be held like this was the height of stupidity and danger, but no matter how loudly her brain shouted at her feet to start walking her body refused to obey.

A thumb was raised up to brush against the underside of her breast and he pressed his groin into the small of her back, letting her feel his arousal. The fire-wielding acrobats became a blur in her vision as her senses all turned in-wards to relish the feel of Helios against her.

She should be like a marble Minoan statue. Unresponsive. Cold. But his touch turned her molten.

Send her to hell, but she rubbed against his arousal. He hissed in her ear, dropping his hand to her hip and gripping it tightly. She could feel his racing heart beating against her back.

Only the loud sound of applause cut through the sensuous fog she'd fallen into.

The show had finished.

The crowd was dispersing.

Blinking hard, aware of Greta searching for her, Amy finally managed to make her body obey, grabbed Helios's hand and pushed it away.

She took a step to distance herself from the security of his hold and drank the last of her mojito.

'Come back with me,' he said. For once, there was no arrogance in his voice.

She kept her eyes from his, not wanting him to see the longing she knew would be written all over her face. 'I can't.'

'You can.'

Greta had spotted them and was heading for them, or rather weaving unsteadily towards them.

'Come back with me,' he repeated.

'No.' She propelled herself down the steps, desperate to be away from him before her vocal cords said the *yes* they so yearned to speak.

He followed her, grabbing her hand when she reached the bottom step and spinning her around.

She waited breathlessly for him to say something, but all he did was stare at her as if he was drinking her in, his thumb brushing little swirls over the inside of her wrist. The message he was sending didn't need words.

Tugging out of his hold, she hurried away before she could respond to his silent request.

Helios pressed a hand to his forehead and growled to his empty bedroom. He'd been back for over an hour and not even his two Long Island iced teas, which had virtually every spirit imaginable in them, had numbed his brain enough to allow him to sleep.

His body still carried remnants of the arousal

that had been unleashed by holding Amy in his arms. One touch was all it had taken. One touch and he'd been fit to burst.

If he'd been one of his ancestors from four hundred years ago he would have marched down the passageway, broken down her door and demanded she give herself to him. As he was a prince of these lands she wouldn't have been allowed to refuse him. She would have had to submit to his will.

But good Queen Athena, Agon's reigning monarch from 1671, had been at the forefront of the abolition of the law which had allowed women to be little more than chattels for the royal family's pleasure.

And even if he could he wouldn't force Amy into his bed. If she came back to him he wanted it to be under her own free will.

He knew she'd returned to the palace. After the fire show she'd disappeared into the throng, and then the last he'd seen of her had been when she'd climbed into one of the waiting palace cars with some of the other live-in staff.

Why was she doing this to him? To *them*? She was as crazy for him as he was for her, and he struggled to understand why she was resisting so hard.

He knew that she wanted to punish him because he had to marry someone else—if he were in her shoes he would probably feel the same way. The mere idea of her with another man was enough to make his blood pressure rise to the point where his veins might explode.

As ashamed as he was to have done so, he'd got his security team to find out who she'd dined with on Saturday night. Leander Soukis, a twenty-two-year-old layabout from a small village on the outskirts of Resina. How Amy had met this man was a mystery. And there was something about their meeting that ground at him.

Never mind that Leander was five years younger than Amy, when Helios distinctly remembered her saying she couldn't relate to younger men, he was also a slight, skinny thing, with a bad reputation. He came from a wealthy family, but that counted for nothing—Leander had been kicked out of three schools and had never held a job for longer than a week. Indeed, he was an ideal candidate for his brother Talos's boxing gym, which he'd opened in order to help disaffected youths, teaching them to channel their anger and giving them a leg up in life.

Why had she gone on a date with him of all people? Had it been her way of proving to Helios that she was serious about their relationship being over? Maybe he should have accepted her resignation rather than let his pride and ego force her into staying. If she was gone from Agon he wouldn't be lying in his bed with a body aching from unfulfilled desire.

But he knew such thoughts were pointless. Amy didn't need to be in his sight to be on his mind. She was there constantly.

And he would bet the palace that right at that moment she was lying in her bed thinking of him.

A soft ping from the security pad on his wall broke through his thoughts.

Jumping out of bed, he pressed a button on it, which brought up the screen issuing the alert. It was from the camera and the sensors in the secret passageway.

Peering closely, he saw a figure moving stealthily along the passageway, getting closer and closer to his room. With his heart in his mouth he watched as she hesitated, and willed her to take the final step and knock on the door.

Amy stared at Helios's door, not quite certain what she was doing or how she had got to this point.

Knowing she was vulnerable to temptation, she'd accepted an invitation to go to one of the other curator's apartments for a drink: a mini-soirée she would usually have loved attending. She'd tried so hard to pull herself out of the trance she'd fallen into, but her contribution to the conversation had been minimal. She couldn't remember a word of it. It was as if she'd been floating above it all, there in body but not in spirit.

She wanted to blame the alcohol, especially the mojitos Helios had given her, but that would have been a lie. It was all down to him.

She'd gone back to her own apartment after just one drink, but before she'd even stepped into her bedroom she'd stopped and stared at the door that led to the secret passageway. Her breaths had shortened as a deep yearning had pulled at her.

Impulse had overridden common sense. She'd unlocked the connecting door and stepped into the passageway in the same dreamlike state she'd ridden back to the palace in, not consciously thinking about where she was going. But now, standing at his door, sanity had pushed its way back through into her mind.

She couldn't do this. It was all wrong.

Closing her eyes, she pressed the palm of her hand to his door, holding it there.

This was as far as she dared go. If she were to knock and he were to answer...

She heard the telltale click of the lock turning.

She snatched her hand away, her breath catching in her throat.

The door opened.

Helios stood in the doorway, naked, nonchalant, as if Amy sneaking up to his room and doing nothing but touch his door was an everyday occurrence. Except the nonchalance was only on the surface. His chest rose and fell in tight judders. His jaw was taut; his nostrils flared. His eyes bore through her as he did nothing but stare.

And then he moved, sending out a hand to wrap around the nape of her neck and pull her to him and over the threshold. As soon as they were in his room he held her firmly and pushed the door shut. He pressed her against it, trapping her.

'Why are you here?' he asked roughly, leaning close enough for his warm, faintly minty breath to touch her skin.

'I don't know,' she whispered.

She *didn't* know. The closest she could come to describing it was her subconscious overriding her resolve. Now, though, the opposite was true. The sensations darting through her had overridden her subconscious and every inch of her had sprung into life. There was not a single atom of her body that wasn't tilting into him, yearning for his kiss, his touch.

'*I* know.'

Then, with a look that suggested he wanted to eat her alive, he brought his mouth to hers and caught her in his kiss.

CHAPTER SEVEN

IF HIS KISS had been the demanding assault she'd anticipated Amy would have been able to resist and push him away. But it wasn't. His lips rested against hers but he made no movement, stilling as if he was breathing in her essence. Amy inhaled deeply in turn, letting the warmth of his breath and the scent of him creep through her pores and inhabit her.

It was as if everything that had happened in the past ten days had been blown away, and with it all the reasons why being alone with him in his apartment and in his arms was all wrong. This was everything she wanted, everything she needed. How could something so wrong feel so *right*?

And now she didn't even want to think about right and wrong. All she wanted was to be in his arms. For ever.

She was the one to part her lips, to dart her

tongue into the darkness of his mouth, to wind her arms around his neck and press into him. She was the one to break the kiss and drag her lips over his stubble-roughened cheeks and jaw and down the strong length of his neck, to run her tongue over the smooth skin, tasting his musky, masculine scent. And she was the one to draw her tongue back up his throat, dig her nails into his scalp and capture his lips with her own.

A tiny sob escaped her mouth when Helios growled and drew his arms around her. He crushed her to him. His lips parted and he kissed her so deeply and so thoroughly that in the breath of an instant she was lost in him.

A large hand dived into her hair whilst his other hand roamed down her back to clutch her bottom, which he squeezed before spreading his palm over her thigh and lifting it. He ground into her and she gasped to feel him huge against her, her underwear the only barrier to stop him entering her there and then.

In a mesh of lips and tongues he pushed her back against the wall, kissing her as if she were a banquet to be feasted on, before pulling away, tugging at her bottom lip painlessly with his teeth as he did so. His chest rising and falling in rapid motion, the palm of one hand held against her chest to still her, Helios lowered himself, pinched the hem of her dress and slowly raised it up. He kissed her stomach as he lifted the dress to her abdomen, his tongue making a trail upwards, through the valley of her breasts, into her neck, until he'd pulled it over her head and thrown it onto the floor.

Amy dug her toes into the hard flooring, her head spinning. Everything inside her blazed as fiercely as the whirling fires she'd seen on the beach. Her skin was alive to his touch. *She* was alive to his touch. Her senses had sprung to life from the very first moment she'd looked at him all those months ago and since then she'd been helpless to switch them off.

He straightened to his full height and stared down at her, his throat moving as his liquid eyes took in her semi-nakedness. He clasped her cheeks in his hands and brought his nose to hers. 'Not being able to touch you or make love to you has driven me crazy,' he said hoarsely. '*You've* driven me crazy.'

She pulled at his hair, wanting to hurt him,

wanting him to experience the pain she'd gone through at the separation she'd had no choice but to force upon them. 'It's hurt me every bit as much as you,' she whispered, bringing her mouth back to his.

Holding her tightly, Helios lifted Amy into his arms, staring at her as he carried her through to his bedroom, delighting in the heightened colour of her cheeks and the dilation of her pupils.

All his dreams and fantasies had come true.

She'd come to him.

He hadn't realised how badly he'd prayed for it until he'd opened the door to her.

But he could still see the last vestiges of doubt and fear ringing in her eyes and he was determined to drive them away.

How could she not know that *this*, here, being together, was exactly how it was supposed to be?

Laying her down on his bed, he kissed her rosebud mouth and inhaled the sweet scent he had come close to believing he would never delight in again. All that separated them was her pretty black underwear. He remembered how once he'd peeled it off with his teeth, in those early hedonistic days when the desire between them had been so great he'd been certain it would *have* to abate. But it had only developed into something deeper, something needier.

Whatever it took, he would keep her in his bed.

As he gazed down, seeing the pulse beating in the arch of her neck, the way she stretched out her legs before raising her pelvis, the urgency grew. *Theos*, but he needed to be inside her.

She raised a lazy hand and pressed it to his chest, then spread her fingers over him, touching him in the way that always filled him with such gratification, as if he were one of the Seven Wonders of the World.

The knowledge that she would explore him in the same manner with which he delighted in exploring her had always been indescribable. There was not a fraction of her he had not tasted and not a fraction of him she had not touched. He would *never* tire of tasting her and making her his.

He slipped a hand behind her back and unclasped her bra, then carefully pulled the straps down her arms, kissing the trail they made and throwing it onto the floor with a flick. With her delectable breasts now bare, the dusky nipples puckered in open invitation, he dipped his head to take one tip in his mouth, groaning as she immediately arched her back to allow him to take more of her in.

Her fingers tugged through his hair as she twisted and writhed beneath him, the urgency in her movements matching the urgency flowing through his veins. She skimmed a hand down over his back before slipping it across his stomach, reaching for him. His attentions now on her other breast, he raised himself a little to make it easier for her to take his erection into her hand, groaning again as she held it in the way she knew he adored, rubbing her thumb over the head and guiding him to the apex of her thighs.

Gritting his teeth and breathing heavily, he kissed her neck and moved her hand away, squeezing her fingers between his own. Immediately she raised her thighs and rubbed against his length, moaning, begging him with soft murmurs.

But there was still the final barrier of her underwear between them.

He kissed her hard on the mouth, then pulled back, drifting his lips down the creaminess of her neck and breasts until he reached her abdomen. There, he pinched the elastic of her underwear between the fingers of both hands and tugged it down, past her thighs and calves and delicate ankles, until she was fully naked before him.

'Please...' she beseeched him, raising her thighs higher and reaching out a hand to touch him. *'Please.'*

Swallowing hard at the sight of her, so full of desire and need for him it made him heady, he guided his erection into her welcoming heat.

He pushed himself in with one long drive and buried his face in her neck, biting gently into the soft skin. And as she gripped him tightly within her he knew without a shadow of a doubt that *this* was where he belonged.

Skin against skin, heartbeat to heartbeat, arms and legs entwined, he made love to her.

And she made love to him.

He could sense the tension within her building, could hear it in the shortening of her breaths, the shallowness of her moans, feel it in the way she gripped his buttocks, deepening his thrusts. And then he felt her pulses pulling at him, pulling him even deeper inside her, her slender frame stilling, her teeth biting into his shoulder.

He didn't want it to end. He wanted it to last for ever, to be locked in her tight sweetness with her legs wrapped around him and her nails digging into his back for eternity...

And then there was no more consciousness. His own climax surged through him, tipping him over a precipice he hadn't known he was on the edge of and exploding in a wash of bright colours that took him to a place he'd never been before.

Amy awoke in the comfort of Helios's embrace, her face pressed against his chest, his arm hooked across her waist, his thigh draped heavily over hers.

Remorse flooded her in an instant.

What had she done?

Everything she'd sworn she wouldn't do had been ripped away in one moment of madness.

She should go. She had to go. She couldn't stay here.

How many times had she awoken in the night in his arms and felt the stirring to make love to him all over again? How many times had she lifted her head a touch and met his kiss? Had him fully hard and inside her in an instant? Too many to count. Sometimes she would wake in the morning and wonder if she'd dreamt their lovemaking in the early hours.

But at this moment Helios's breathing was deep and even. If she was careful she might be able to sneak out without him waking. Then she could flee to her apartment, pack a suitcase and check into a hotel. That was it. That was what she had to do.

Because she couldn't stay here—not now when she knew how hopeless she was at resisting him.

She'd tried so hard to stay away.

Oh, God, what had she *done*?

She could dress it up any way she liked but she'd given in to temptation, and now the ecstasy of being back in his arms had gone, replaced with an acrid taste in her mouth and a gutful of guilt.

She had to leave. Right now.

Carefully, after stealthily slipping out of his arms, she edged her way out of the bed, holding her breath until her feet touched the floor.

Scrambling, half-blind in the dark, she found

her dress thrown across an armchair. She had no idea where her underwear had got to and was in too much of a panic to escape to hunt for it for long. She shrugged her dress on and, fearful of choking on the swell rising in her chest, tiptoed to the door.

'You wouldn't be running away, would you?'

Helios watched as Amy's silhouette froze at the bedroom door. Switching on the bedside light, he propped himself up on an elbow as she slowly turned around to face him with wide, pain-filled taupe eyes. To see her mussed-up hair and her beautiful face contorted in such misery... Something sharp pierced him.

'I'm sorry,' she whimpered. 'I know it's cowardly to sneak away.'

'Then why are you?'

'I shouldn't be here. We shouldn't have...' Her voice tailed away and she looked down at the floor.

'Made love?' he supplied.

She gave a tiny nod. 'It was wrong. All wrong.'

'It felt damn right to me.'

'I know.' She gave a sudden bark of harsh laughter and her eyes flashed. 'It's what I keep thinking. How can something so wrong feel so right?'

'If it feels so right then how can it be wrong?' he countered.

'It just is. You're getting *married*.'

That little fact was something that constantly played on his mind. Only being in Amy's arms had driven it and the accompanying nausea away.

Tightness coiled in his stomach. Throwing off the covers, he climbed out of bed and strode over to her, slamming his hand on the door to prevent her from escaping.

He spoke slowly, trying to think the words through before he vocalised them, knowing that one wrong word would make her flee whether or not he barricaded the door. 'Amy, I might be getting married, but it's *you* I want.'

'We've been through this before. It doesn't matter what you want or what I want. It doesn't change the reality of the situation. Tonight was a mistake that can't be repeated.'

'Running away won't change anything either. Admit it, *matakia mou*. You and I belong together.'

Her jaw clenched in response.

'So what are you going to do?' he asked scathingly, leaning closer to her ashen face. 'Run away and start a relationship with Leander? Is that how you intend to prove we're over?'

'How do you know about Leander?' She shook her head and took a deep inhalation. 'Don't answer that. I can guess.'

He felt no guilt for seeking information about her date. Helios looked out for those he cared for. 'He's too young for you. I know you, Amy. You don't need a boy. You need—'

'He's my brother,' she snapped suddenly, angry colour flushing her cheeks.

Her declaration momentarily stunned him into silence. Stepping back to look at her properly, he dragged a hand through his hair. 'But Leander is from Agon. Your brothers are English, like you...'

'I'm only half-English.'

'Your parents are English.' *Weren't* they? Wasn't this something they had talked about...?

'My father's English. Elaine—my mum— didn't give birth to me. My birth mother's from Agon.'

How had he not known this?

Amy must have sensed the direction his mind was travelling in. 'Do you remember once asking me how I'd developed such an obsession and a love for your country?'

'You said it was… You never gave a proper answer…' Realisation dawned on him as he thought back to that conversation, months ago, when they had first started sleeping together. She'd brushed his question aside.

'And you never pursued it.' She shook her head in a mixture of sadness and anger.

'I didn't know there was anything to pursue. I'm not a mind reader.'

'I'm sorry.' She gave a helpless shrug. 'A huge part of me wanted to tell you, and ask for your help in finding her, but I knew that confiding in you would change the nature of our relationship.'

'What would have changed?' he asked, completely perplexed.

From the first the chemistry between them had been off the charts. Making love to Amy had always felt different from the way it had felt with his other lovers. He'd never felt the urge to ask her to leave at night—he liked sharing his space with her, this incredibly sexy woman with a brain the size of a watermelon. He loved it that she could teach him things he didn't know about his own country.

To learn now that she had *roots* in his country…

'I didn't keep any secrets from you,' he added, his head reeling.

'Apart from throwing a party to find a wife?'

He inhaled deeply. Yes, the real purpose of the ball *was* something he'd kept from her for as long as he could. But this information was on a different scale. He'd known Amy had kept a part of herself sheltered from him, but he'd had no idea it was something so fundamental.

Her eyes held his. 'I was scared.'

Another stabbing pain lanced him. 'Of me?'

'Of what you would think of me. At least I was in the beginning.' Her voice lowered to a whisper. 'And I was scared because you and I came with time constraints. We had a fixed marker for when we would end, we both knew that. We both held things back.'

'I never held anything back.'

'Didn't you?' There was no challenge in her

eyes, just a simple question. 'Helios, I couldn't take the risk of what we had developing into something more—of us becoming closer. We can't be together for ever. I was trying to pro-tect myself.'

For an age he stared at her, wishing he could see into her mind, wishing he could shake her… wishing that everything could be different.

'Do not go anywhere,' he said, turning his back to her and striding to his dressing room. 'You and I are going to talk, and this is not a conversation to have naked. We're long past the point of keeping secrets from each other.'

While Helios slipped on a pair of boxers Amy used the few moments alone to catch her thoughts before he reappeared.

It wasn't long enough.

She pressed her back tightly against the door, her vocal cords too constricted for speech.

'I mean it, Amy,' he said with a hard look in his eye. 'You're not going anywhere until we've talked this through.'

'What's the point?' she asked, her voice hoarse.

'If your history is what's stopping us from being together then I damn well deserve to know the truth.' He strolled back to the bed and sat in the middle of it, his back resting against the headboard. 'Now, come here.'

What an unholy mess. It had never been supposed to end like this. Her memories of her time with him were supposed to be filled with wonder, not sorrow and despair. Losing him wasn't supposed to *hurt*.

She perched on the end of the bed and twisted to face him. Blowing out a puff of air, she gazed at the ceiling.

'My father had an affair with the au pair. She dumped me on him when I was two weeks old and has wanted nothing to do with me since. Her husband and her parents don't know I exist.'

CHAPTER EIGHT

OTHER THAN A slight shake of his head and a tightening of his lips, Helios gave no response.

'My birth mother had me when she was nineteen. I know very little about her—she didn't work for them for long.'

'When you say *for them*…?'

'My parents. My mum—as in the woman who raised me—was pregnant and had a three-year-old son when they employed Neysa, my birth mother, as an au pair. She quit after a couple of months but then turned up at my dad's workplace seven months later and left me with the receptionist.'

Amy studied Helios's reaction carefully. She no longer really feared, as she had at the beginning of their relationship, that he would think any less of her, but nagging doubts remained. Cruel words spoken in the playground still haunted her, clouding her judgement.

'You must have been one ugly baby for your own mum to dump you.'

'Do you have 666 marked on the back of your head?'

'Your real mum's a slut.'

She'd had to force herself to rise above it and pretend the taunts didn't affect her when in reality they had burned. For years she had tortured herself, wondering if the taunts held the ring of truth. For years she'd tried to live a life as pure as the driven snow to *prove* she wasn't intrinsically bad.

For years she'd wondered how Elaine—to her mind, her mum—could even bring herself to look at her.

Helios stared at her as if she'd just told him that all the scientists and even physics itself were wrong and the world was actually flat.

'Did she leave a note?' he asked quietly. 'Give a reason?'

'Her note to my father said only that I was his and that she couldn't keep me.'

'So your father had an affair with the au pair when your mum was pregnant? And they're still together?'

She nodded. 'God knows how Mum found it in her to forgive him but she did, and she raised me as her own.'

Helios shook his head, amazement in his eyes. 'She raised you with her own children?'

'Yes. Danny was born five months before me. We were in the same school year.'

He closed his eyes with a wince. 'That must have been difficult.'

'At times it was horrendous—especially at secondary school. But we coped.'

Amy's existence could have caused major friction between her and her siblings, but both Danny and their older brother, Neil, had always been fiercely protective of her, particularly during their teenage years.

'Did you always know?'

'Not when I was a young child. My family was my family. Danny being five months older than me…it was just a fact of our lives. Neil always knew I was only his half-sister but, again, it was just a fact of our lives and something he assumed was normal. My parents never mentioned it so he didn't either. Then we got older and other kids started asking questions…Mum told me the truth when I was ten.'

She shuddered at the memory of that sudden realisation that her whole life had been a lie.

'She'd been waiting until I was old enough to understand.'

It had been the most significant moment of Amy's life. It would have been easy to feel as if her whole world had caved in, but Danny and Neil had simply shrugged it off and continued to treat her as they always had—as their sister. That, more than anything, had made it easier to cope with.

'Did you not have *any* idea you weren't hers?'

'Not in the slightest. She loved me. Any resentment was hidden.'

'What about your father? Where does he fit in with all this?'

'He left it to my mum to tell me. When it came out he carried on as normal, trying to pretend nothing had changed.'

But of course everything had changed. *She'd* changed. How could she not? Everything she'd thought she knew about herself had been a lie.

She looked back at Helios, wanting him to understand. 'When I was told the truth it became important, I guess, to pretend that nothing had changed. They still treated me the same. They still scolded me when I was naughty. My mum still tucked me up in bed and kissed me good-night. Outwardly, nothing did change.'

'And how does she feel about you being here now, trying to find your birth mother?'

'She understands. She's adopted herself—I think that's why she was able to raise me without blaming me for the sins of my birth mother. She knows what the urge to find out who you really are is like.'

Her mum had encouraged Amy's quest to learn all there was to know about Agon. She'd been the one to take her to the library to seek out books on Agon and Minoan culture and to record any television documentary that featured the island. So encouraging had she been that a part of Amy had been scared her mum *wanted* her to go to Agon and stay there. She'd been afraid that she wanted to get rid of the living proof of her husband's infidelity, that all the love she had bestowed on Amy had only been an act.

But Amy couldn't deny that she'd seen the apprehension in her mum's eyes when she'd left for Agon. Since she'd been on the island she'd received more daily calls and messages than she had when she'd first left home for university. Was she secretly worried that Amy would abandon her for Neysa...?

Secretly worried or not, wanting to get rid of her or not, being adopted herself meant her mum had first-hand experience of knowing what it was like to feel a part of you was missing. Helios had always known exactly who he was. There hadn't been a single day of his life when he hadn't known his place in the world or his destiny.

'She sounds like a good woman.'

'She is. She's lovely.' And she was. Loving and selfless. Amy knew her fears were irrational, but she had no control over them. They were still there, taunting her, in the deepest recesses of her mind.

'So why do you want to meet your birth mother?' Helios asked, puzzled that Amy could want *anything* to do with someone who'd caused such pain and destruction. 'She abandoned you and destroyed your mum's trust.'

She looked away. 'I don't want a relationship with her. I just… I want to know what she looks like. Do I look like her? Because the only thing I've inherited from my dad is his nose. And I want to know why she did what she did.'

'Even if the truth hurts you?' If her birth mother was anything like her layabout son, he would guess she'd abandoned Amy for purely selfish reasons.

'I've been hurt every day of my life since I learned the truth of my conception,' she said softly. 'I know there are risks to meeting her, but I can't spend the rest of my life wondering.'

'Has your father not been able to fill in any of the gaps for you?'

'Not really. He doesn't like to talk about her— he's still ashamed of his behaviour. He's a scientist, happily stuck in a laboratory all day, and what he did was completely out of character.' She gave a sad smile. 'Even if he did want to talk about it there's not much for him to say. He hardly knew her. She was hired on a recommendation from one of Dad's colleagues who left his research company before I was dumped on him. All he and my mum knew was that Neysa—my birth mother—was from Agon and had come to England for a year to improve her English.'

And so the Greens had allowed a stranger into their home, with no foreknowledge of the havoc that would be wreaked on them.

'Everything else I've learned since I came here,' she added wistfully. 'Greta has helped me.'

But she hadn't confided in *him* or approached him for help.

Helios tried to imagine the pain and angst she'd been living with during all the nights they'd shared together. She hadn't breathed a word of it, although she must have known he was in the best position to help her.

'How's your parents' marriage now?'

Amy shrugged. 'When it all happened I was still a newborn baby. They patched their marriage up as best they could for the sake of us kids. They seem happy. I don't think my dad ever cheated again, but who knows?'

'My mother was a good woman too,' he said.

He was realising that Amy was right in her assertion that they had both kept things hidden. Both of them had kept parts of their lives locked away. And now it was time to unlock them.

'And my father was also a philanderer. But, unlike your father, mine never showed any penitence. The opposite, in fact.'

Her taupe eyes widened a touch but she didn't answer, just waited for him to continue in his own time.

'My father was hugely unfaithful—to be honest, he was a complete bastard. And my mother was incredibly jealous. To shut her up when she questioned him about his infidelities he would hit her. She deserved better than him.'

This was not a subject he'd ever discussed with anyone outside of his family. His father's infidelities were well documented, but his violence... that was something they'd all closed ranks on. Being the sons of such a vicious, narcissistic man was not something any of the brothers had found it easy to reconcile themselves with.

'I'm sorry,' Amy said, shaking her head slowly as if trying to take in his words. 'Did you know it was going on? The violence, I mean?'

'Only on an instinctual level. It was only ever a feeling.'

'How was *your* relationship with your father?' she asked quietly.

He grimaced as decades-old memories flooded him. 'I was the apple of his eye. He adored me, to the point that he excluded my brothers. It felt good, being the "special" one, but I also felt much guilt about it too. He was cruel—especially to Theseus. My mother struggled to make him treat us all fairly.'

Amy didn't say anything, just stared at him with haunted eyes.

'I was a child when they died. My memories are tainted by everything I learned after he'd gone, but I remember the looks he would give my mother when she stood up for Theseus or made a pointed remark about his other women. I would feel sick with worry for her, but he was always careful to make sure I was out of sight and earshot before hitting her. It got worse once I left for boarding school,' he continued. 'With me gone, he didn't have to hide it any more.'

'You surely don't blame yourself for that?'

'Not any more. But I did when I first learned the truth.' He met her gaze. 'It took me a long time to truly believe I couldn't have stopped him even if I had known. But, like you when your life fell apart, I was a child. Talos tried to stop it—

that last day, before my parents were driven to the Greek Embassy and their car crashed, Talos was there, right in the middle of it. He got hurt himself in the crossfire.'

'Oh, the poor boy. That must have been horrendous for him.'

'It screwed up his ideas of marriage. He has no intention of ever marrying.'

'Not an option for you,' she said softly.

'No.' He shook his head for emphasis. 'Nor for Theseus. The security of our family and our island rests in our hands. But I swear this now— my parents' marriage will not be mine.'

'What if it was an option?' she asked suddenly, straightening. 'What if you'd been born an ordinary person? Who would you be now?'

'I don't know.' And he didn't. 'It's not something I've ever thought about.'

'Really?'

'Theseus spent most of his life fighting his birthright and all it brought him was misery. Why rail against something you have no control over? I had no control over my conception, just as I had no control over my parents' marriage or their deaths. My destiny is what it is, and I've always known and accepted that. I am who I am and I'm comfortable with that.'

It was only in recent weeks that the destiny he'd always taken for granted had gained a more acrid tang.

During their conversation Amy had moved fully back onto the bed and was now facing him, hugging her knees. Reaching forward, he took her left foot into his hands and gently tugged at it so it rested on his lap.

A strange cathartic sensation blew through him, and with it a sense of release. His father's violence and complete disrespect to his mother were things that he'd locked away inside, not wanting to give voice to the despicable actions he and his brothers felt tainted by. But Amy was the last person who would judge a child for the sins of its parents. In that respect they shared something no other could understand.

'The main reason I selected Catalina is because she has no illusions about what our marriage will be,' he said, massaging Amy's foot. 'She has been groomed from birth to marry someone of equal stature. I will be King, but I will never be like my father. Marrying Catalina guarantees that she will never expect more than I can give.'

'But your mother was a princess before she married your father.'

His mouth twisted. 'Their marriage was arranged before she could walk. She grew up knowing she would marry my father and she built an ideal in her head of what their marriage would be like. She loved him all her life and, God help her, she was doomed to disappointment. The only person my father loved was himself. Catalina doesn't love me any more than I love her. There will be no jealousy. She has no expectations of fidelity.'

'Has she said that?' Amy asked doubtfully.

'Her only expectation is that I be respectful to her and discreet, and that is something I will always be. Whatever happens in the future, I will *never* inflict on her or on anyone the pain my father inflicted on my mother.'

'I know you wouldn't hurt her intentionally. But, Helios, what she says now...it doesn't mean she'll feel the same way once you've exchanged your vows.' Amy closed her eyes and sighed. 'And it doesn't change how I feel about it. I won't be the other woman. Marriage vows should be sacred.'

Helios placed her foot gently onto the bed before pouncing, grabbing her hands and pinning her beneath him.

Breathing heavily, she turned her face away from him.

'Look at me,' he commanded.

'No.'

'Amy, look at me.' He loosened his hold only when she reluctantly turned her face back to him. 'You are not Neysa—you are Elaine's daughter, with all *her* goodness. Catalina is not your mother. Nor is she mine. And I am *not* my father. The mistakes they all made and the pain they caused are not ours to repeat. That's something neither of us would ever allow to happen.'

He came closer so his lips were a breath away from hers.

'And I'm not married yet.'

Her eyes blazed back at him, desire and misery fighting in them. He leaned down and placed a kiss to her neck, smoothing his hand over her breasts and down to her thighs. He inched the hem of her dress up and slid between her legs.

'Neither of us are ready for this to end. Why deny ourselves when my vows are still to be made and we're not hurting anyone?'

Amy fought the familiar tingles and sensations spreading through her again as the need to touch him and hold him grew stronger than ever. How was it possible to go from wanting to wrap him in her arms, to chase away what she knew were dreadful memories for him, to sensual need in the blink of an eye?

She writhed beneath him. Her words came in short breaths. 'I can't think when you're doing this to me.'

'Then don't think. Just feel. And accept that we're not over.'

In desperation she grabbed at his hair, forcing *him* to look at *her*. 'But you've made a commitment.'

'A commitment that won't be fulfilled for two months.' He slid inside her, penetrating as deep as he could go.

She gasped as pleasure filled her.

'Until then,' he continued, his voice becoming heavy as he began to move, 'you are mine and I am yours.'

Amy tightened her hold around Helios, wishing she didn't feel so complete with his weight upon her and his steadying breaths softly tickling the skin of her neck. She was a fool for him. More so than she could have imagined.

They'd laid their pasts bare to each other and the effect had been the very thing she'd been scared of. She felt closer to him, as if an invisible emotional bond had wrapped itself around them.

He finally shifted his weight off her and she rolled over and burrowed into his arms.

'Don't even think about trying to sneak out,' he said sleepily.

'I won't.' She gave a soft, bittersweet laugh. Her resolve had deserted her. Those bonds had cocooned her so tightly to him she could no longer envisage cutting them. Not yet. Not until she really had to. 'You and I...'

'What?' he asked, after her words had tailed off.

'No one can know. Please. Everyone who knew we were together knows we split up. I couldn't bear for them to think we're having an affair behind the Princess's back.'

When they'd been together originally Helios had made no secret of her place in his life. She might not have accompanied him to official functions, or been recognised as his official girlfriend, but she had been his almost constant companion within the palace.

She'd spent far more time in his apartment than she had in her own, and whenever he had come into the museum he would seek her out. He would touch her—not sexually…he at least had a sense of propriety when it came to *that* in public…but he would rest his hand in the small of her back, lean close to her, all the little tells of a possessive man staking his claim on the woman in his life. And if work or duty took him away from the palace she would be the one to look after Benedict.

It had only been on the inside, emotionally, that they had been separated. But not any more. At this moment she didn't think she had ever felt as close to anyone in her life.

'Discretion will be my new name,' he acquiesced.

'And when you marry you will let me go.'

He stilled.

Watching for his reaction, she saw his eyes open. 'That gives you two months to find my replacement,' she whispered. 'I want to know that you'll release me from the palace and from your life. I appreciate it means bringing my contract to an early end, but I don't think I'll be able to cope with living and working here knowing it's the Princess you're sleeping with.'

When he married their bonds would be destroyed.

He breathed deeply, then nodded. 'I can agree to that. But until then...'

'Until then I am yours.'

CHAPTER NINE

HELIOS CLICKED ON Leander Soukis's profile and stared hard at it. There was something about the young man's chin and the colouring of his hair that reminded him of Amy, but that was the only resemblance he could see. How could Amy share half her DNA with this layabout? Amy was one of the hardest workers he'd ever met, which, in a palace and museum full of overachievers was saying something.

And how she could be from the loins of Neysa Soukis was beyond his comprehension. Helios had done his homework on Amy's birth mother and what he had learned had not given him hope of a happy ending.

Neysa was a social climber. Approaching fifty, she still had a refined beauty. She had a rich older husband, who doted on her, and a comfortable lifestyle. Helios vaguely recalled meeting her husband at a palace function a few years back. Neysa had married him when she was twenty-one, less than two years after having Amy. Why she hadn't confessed to having had a child he could only speculate upon, but his guess was that it had nothing to do with shame and everything to do with fear. No doubt she'd been scared of losing the wealth that came with her marriage.

Neysa had put money before her own flesh and blood. If Helios had his way Amy wouldn't be allowed within a mile's radius of the woman. But he understood how deep blood could go. That morning he'd met his nephew for the first time. He'd felt an instant thump in his heart.

This little boy, this walking, talking dark-haired creation was a part of *him*. His family. His bloodline. He was a Kalliakis, and Helios had felt the connection on an emotional level.

It might break her heart in the process, but Amy deserved to know her bloodline too.

Whether the Soukis family deserved *her* was another matter...

If they did break her heart he would be there to pick up the pieces and help her through it, just as Amy had been there with a comforting embrace whenever the pain of his grandfather's illness had caught him in its grip.

Thinking quickly, Helios drafted a private message. If having a decree from the heir to the throne didn't motivate Leander to bring his mother and half-sister together, nothing would.

'Amy, you're late for your meeting.'

'What meeting?' she asked Pedro in surprise, looking down at him from her position on a stepladder, from where she was adjusting the portraits lining the first exhibition room. She wanted them to be hung perfectly, not so much as a millimetre out of alignment.

The museum and the palace tours had been closed to visitors all week in order to prepare for the Gala. As a result the palace and its grounds were in a state of absolute frenzy, with helicopters landing on the palace helipad on a seemingly constant basis. And the Gala was still a day away!

She'd never known the palace to be such a hive of activity. There was a buzz about the place, and information and gossip were being dripped in from so many sources, including the more serious museum curators, whose heads were usually stuck in historical tomes, that it seemed like a spreading infection.

The Orchestre National de Paris had arrived to great fanfare, a world-famous circus troupe had been spotted lurking in the grounds, the gardens had been closed off to allow even more blooms to be planted... Everywhere Amy went something magical was occurring.

The exhibition was to all intents and purposes ready for the *very* exclusive private tour that would be conducted after the pre-Gala lunch. Another, less exclusive tour would take place on Sunday, and the museum and exhibition would open to the public on Monday. From then on it really would be all systems go. Ticket demand had exceeded expectations.

She wanted it to be perfect—not just because of her professional pride, but also for Helios, his grandfather and his brothers.

'Your meeting with Helios,' Pedro said. 'He's waiting for you in his private offices.'

'Oh.' She rubbed at her lips, avoiding Greta's curious stare, willing them both not to notice the flames licking at her face.

Helios had been as good as his word. No one knew they were sharing a bed again, not even Greta. It wasn't just guilt preventing Amy from confiding in her friend, but the feeling that what she and Helios had now was just too intimate to share.

'Yes. Yes, I remember.'

Excusing herself politely, still not meeting their eyes, Amy hurried away. When she'd kissed Helios goodbye that morning, before coming to work, she'd assumed that he would be flat-out busy all day. His itinerary had given her a headache just looking at it. A frisson ran up her spine as she imagined what he might be wanting from her. She doubted very much that it had anything to do with the museum.

Helios's private offices were attached to his private apartment. Getting there was a trek in itself. She could cut through her own apartment and use their secret passageway, but during daylight hours it wasn't feasible, not when this was an 'official' meeting, even if it would shave ten minutes off her walk.

The usual courtiers guarded his quarters. They were expecting her and opened the door without any questions. She stepped inside, into a large reception area. The door to the left led to his apartment. She turned the handle of the door to the right.

Talia, Helios's private secretary, rose to greet her, a pastry in her hand. 'Hello, Amy,' she said with a welcoming smile. Usually immaculately presented, today Talia had a wild-eyed, frazzled look about her. 'He's expecting you.'

Did Talia suspect Amy and Helios had resumed their relationship? Did *anyone* suspect?

Amy smiled back politely. 'How are things?'

Talia crossed her eyes and pulled a face. 'Busy. This is the first time we've stopped all day.' She pressed a key on one of her desk phones. 'Despinis Green is here,' she said.

'Send her in,' came the response.

Amy found Helios sitting behind his sprawling desk with Benedict, his black Labrador, snoozing beside him. Benedict cocked an ear and opened his eyes when she walked into the office, then promptly went back to sleep.

'Take a seat,' Helios said politely, his eyes following her every movement with a certain knowingness.

As soon as the door was closed and they had some privacy he rose from his chair and stepped round the desk to take her in his arms.

'Was there a reason you made up a non-existent meeting other than to make out with me in your office?' she asked with bemusement when they came up for air.

His hands forked through her hair and he kissed her again. 'The French Ambassador's flight was slightly delayed, giving me an unexpected half-hour window.'

'It took me that long to get here,' she said teasingly.

'I know.' He gave a mock sigh. 'I suppose a few kisses are better than nothing.'

She laughed and rested her head against his chest. 'Should I go now?'

He looked at his watch. 'Five minutes.'

'That's hardly any time.'

Not that she could do anything more than share a few kisses with him in his office, with Talia on the other side of the door and the palace full of Very Important People who all demanded his time. How he kept his good humour was a mystery…

'There's always time for kissing,' he said, tilting her chin up so he could nuzzle into her cheek. 'Especially as I won't get the chance to touch you again for at least another ten hours...' Before she could get too comfortable, however, he stepped away. 'To answer your original question—yes, I did have an ulterior motive for seeing you other than the insatiable need to kiss you.'

She rolled her eyes.

'Before I tell you...I don't want you to think I've been interfering.'

'What have you interfered with?'

'I told you, I'm not interfering. I'm helping,' he added, with a deliberate display of faux innocence.

'What have you done?'

His features became serious. 'I've been in contact with your birth mother.'

Her heart almost stopped. 'And?' she asked breathlessly.

'She has agreed to meet you in a neutral place on Monday.'

She shook her head, trying to clear the sudden buzzing that had started in her brain at this unexpected development.

'Are you angry with me?'

'No. Of course not.' She wrapped her arms around him and breathed him in. His scent was so very reassuring. 'It's in your nature to take charge and boss people around.'

He laughed and rubbed his hands down her back. 'I wrote to her in my capacity as your boss. And in my capacity as her Prince.'

'It's amazing how people are able to do an about-turn on the basis of a simple word from you.'

'It certainly is,' he agreed cheerfully.

'If I were a princess I would throw my weight around everywhere.'

He pulled back and tapped her on the nose. 'No, you wouldn't... And I don't throw my weight around,' he continued, feigning injury.

She grinned. 'You don't need to.' Stepping onto her toes, she pressed a kiss to his lips. 'Thank you.'

'Don't thank me yet—there are no guarantees the meeting will go well.'

She shrugged. 'Having met Leander, I have no expectations. I don't want to be part of her family or cause trouble for her. I just want to meet her.'

'Just…be careful. Don't build your hopes up.'

'I won't,' she promised, knowing his warning came from a place of caring, just as his interference had. If their roles had been reversed she would be warning him too.

'Good. I'll email you the details.'

'Thank you.'

One of the landlines on his desk buzzed. Sighing, Helios disentangled his arms from around her and pressed a button. 'Yes?'

'The French contingent have landed and are expected in twenty minutes.'

'Thank you. I'll leave in a moment to greet them.' Disconnecting the call, he shook his head and grimaced. 'One more kiss before duty calls?'

Obliging him, Amy leaned closer, raised herself onto the tips of her toes and brought her mouth to his, giving him one last, lingering kiss before he broke away with a rueful smile.

'I'll see you later and we'll do a *lot* more than kissing,' he said, then strode to the office door and opened it.

'The Koreans will be arriving within the hour,' Talia called as he walked past her.

He shook his head. 'Whose idea was it to have so many guests arrive a day early?'

'Yours,' Talia said, her expression deadpan.

'The next time I come up with such an idea you're welcome to chop my hands off.'

Hoping her demeanour was as nonchalant as his, Amy said goodbye to Talia. When she stepped out into the corridor Helios had already gone.

Gala day had arrived.

If Helios had been busy the day before, it was nothing compared to today. His whole morning had been spent meeting and greeting guests and making sure everything was running perfectly.

This was a day he'd looked forward to. No one could organise an occasion better than the Agon palace staff and he always enjoyed celebrating the events they hosted. He was immensely proud of his family and his island, and never turned down an opportunity to discuss its virtues with interesting people.

With his grandfather's situation as it was, he'd

expected the day to feel bittersweet, with the joy of celebrating the great man's life certain to be shadowed by the knowledge that it would soon be ending.

What Helios hadn't expected was to feel flat.

There was a strange lethargy within him which he was fighting against. Merely shaking hands and making eye contact felt like an effort. His mouth didn't want to smile. He hadn't even found the energy to be disappointed by the news that the solo violinist Talos had been working so closely with would not be able to perform due to severe stage fright.

One bright spot had been the unveiling of his grandfather's biography, which he and his brothers had looked through with their grandfather privately before the pre-Gala lunch. To see the man who'd raised them make his peace with Theseus had warmed him. And King Astraeus had surprised them all by revealing that he knew about Theseus's son and his plans to marry the boy's mother, and had given his blessing.

These were all things that should have had Helios slapping his brothers' backs and calling for a glass of champagne.

They'd gone through to the lunch together. Again, he should have revelled in the occasion, but the food had tasted like cardboard, the champagne flat on his tongue.

His fiancée, who'd arrived with her father and her brother, Helios's old school friend, had sat next to him throughout the lunch. He'd had to force the pleasantries expected of him. When Catalina's father, the King of Monte Cleure, had commented about the announcement of their engagement it had taken all his willpower not to slam his knife into the table and shout, *To hell with the announcement!*

And now, with the lunch over, the clock was ticking furiously fast towards the time when he would make his engagement official to the world.

First, though, it was time for his grandfather to have a very exclusive viewing of his exhibition. It would include just the King and his three grandsons. Above everything else occurring that day, taking his grandfather to the exhibition created in his honour was the part Helios had most been looking forward to. The biography was the culmination of Theseus's hard work—a tangible acknowledgement of his love and pride—and this exhibition was the pinnacle of his own.

With his brothers by his side, Helios and a couple of courtiers now led his grandfather out into the palace grounds and along the footpath that led to the museum.

The joy and pride he'd anticipated feeling in this moment had been squashed by a very real sense of dread. And when they arrived at the museum doors he understood where the dread had come from.

Amy, Pedro and four other staff members closely involved in the exhibition were there to greet them at the museum's entrance. All were wearing their official uniforms and not a single hair was out of place. This was their big moment as much as his.

Talos wheeled their grandfather up to the line of waiting staff so they could be spoken to in turn. When they reached Amy the thuds in Helios's heart became a painful racket.

This was the first time she would meet his family. It would also be the last.

Bracing himself, he said, 'This is the exhibition curator, Amy Green. She's on secondment from England to organise it all.'

Not looking at Helios, Amy curtsied. 'It is an honour to meet you, Your Majesty.'

'The honour is mine,' his grandfather replied with that wheeze in his voice Helios didn't think he would ever get used to. 'I've been looking forward to seeing this exhibition. Are you my tour guide?'

Her eyes darted to Pedro, who, as Head of Museum, was supposed to take the role of the King's guide.

Sensing her dilemma, Helios stepped in. 'Despinis Green would be delighted to be your guide. Let's get you inside and we can make a start.'

Inside the main exhibition room the four King Astraeus statues were lined up on their plinths. The sculptor of the fourth, which was covered and ready for unveiling, awaited his introduction to the King. When that was done, and the official photographers were in position, in a hushed silence the cover was removed and the King was able to see his own youthful image portrayed in marble for the first time.

For the longest, stillest moment the King simply stared at it, drinking in the vibrant, enigmatic quality of his statue. There was a collective exhalation of breath when he finally spoke of his delight and reached out a wizened hand to touch his own marble foot.

It was a moment Amy knew would be shown in all the world's press.

From there, the group progressed through to the rest of the exhibition.

The thought of being the King's personal tour guide should have had Amy in fits of terror, but it was a welcome relief. She had to concentrate so hard to keep up with etiquette and protocol that she could almost act as if Helios meant nothing to her other than as her boss.

But only almost.

After the King had examined and admired all of the military exhibits, they moved through to the room dedicated to his marriage to Queen Rhea, who had died five years previously. It was heartbreaking and yet uplifting to see the King's reaction first-hand.

Their wedding outfits had been carefully placed on mannequins and secured inside a glass cabinet. Queen Rhea's wedding dress was one of the most beautiful creations Amy had ever been privileged to handle, covered as it was with over ten thousand tiny diamonds and crystals.

King Astraeus gazed at it with moist eyes before saying to her, 'My Queen looked beautiful that day.'

Amy murmured her agreement. On the opposite wall hung the official wedding portrait. Queen Rhea had been a beauty by anyone's standards, but on that particular day there had been a glow about her that shone through the portrait and every photo that had been taken.

What would it be like to have a marriage such as theirs? Her own parents' marriage had seemed mostly happy, but once Amy had learned of her true parentage her memories had become slanted.

Her father's infidelity, although mostly never spoken of, remained a scar. Danny knew their father had cheated on his mother whilst she'd carried him. Neil knew their father had cheated on his mother back when he'd still been talking in broken sentences. They might love Amy as a true sister, and have nothing to do with anyone who saw things differently, but their relationship with their father bordered on uncomfortable. They didn't trust him and neither did Amy. She loved him very much, but the nagging doubts remained. When they'd still been living at home, and he'd been kept late at work, although they'd never said anything they'd all wondered if his excuses were true. And as for her mum…

To anyone looking in, their marriage would seem complete. They laughed together and enjoyed each other's company. But then Amy thought of the times she'd caught her mum going through her father's phone when she'd thought no one was looking and knew the pain she'd gone through had never fully mended. Once trust had been broken it was incredibly hard to repair.

King Astraeus and Queen Rhea's marriage had bloomed into that rarest of things: enduring, faithful love. The kind of love Amy longed to have. The kind of love she could never have when the man she loved was going to marry someone else…

The truth hit her like a bolt of lightning.

She *did* love him.

And as the revelation hit her so did another truth of equal magnitude.

She was going to lose him.

But he'd never been hers to lose, so she already had.

There was nothing for her to hold on to for support. All she could do was keep a grip on herself and wait for the wave of anguish to pass.

The only man she could ever be happy with, the only man she could ever find enduring love with, the only man she had trusted with the truth of her conception... He was marrying someone else. The happy ending she'd always hoped she would one day have would never be hers.

When she dared to look at Helios she found his gaze on her, a question resonating from his liquid eyes. He was as sensitive to her changes of mood as she was to his.

She forced a smile and straightened her posture, doing her best to resume her professional demeanour. Whatever personal torment she might have churning inside her, she still had a job to do.

This was King Astraeus's big day, one he'd spent eighty-seven years of duty and sacrifice working towards. This was his moment. It was also Helios's and his brothers' moment too. The three Princes loved their grandfather, and this day was as much for them to show their appreciation of him as to allow their great nation to celebrate. She wouldn't do anything to detract from the culmination of all their hard work.

Amy kept her head up throughout the rest of the tour, but as soon as it was over she fled, using the pretext of needing to change her outfit for the Gala. Thankfully all the other staff wanted to change too, so saw nothing strange in her behaviour.

Finally alone in her apartment, she sank onto the edge of her bed and cradled her head in her hands. The tears that had threatened to pour throughout the exhibition tour had now become blocked. The emotions raging inside her had compacted so tightly and painfully that the release she needed wouldn't come.

The truth of her feelings and the hopelessness of her love had hit her so hard she had shut down inside.

CHAPTER TEN

FIVE THOUSAND PEOPLE were settled in the amphitheatre, watching the Gala, enjoying the multitude of performances taking turns on the stage, the glorious sunshine, the food and the drink.

Amy, sitting with the rest of the museum staff, tried to enjoy what was a truly spectacular occasion. A world-famous operatic duo from the US had just completed a medley of songs from *The Phantom of the Opera*, and now a Russian ballet troupe had taken to the stage, holding everyone spellbound.

When they were done, the compère came bounding back on. 'Ladies and gentlemen, boys and girls, in a small addition to our official programme, I am proud to welcome to the stage His Royal Highness, Prince Helios.'

Huge cheers broke out around the amphitheatre as the crowd rose to their feet to applaud the popular Prince.

Amy's stone-filled feet moved of their own accord and she stood too. The coldness rippling through her was such that it felt as if someone had injected ice into her veins. All the hairs on her arms had sprung upright. Nausea didn't churn—no, it turned and twisted, as if her stomach had been locked in a superfast waltzer. And yet the tightness in her chest remained, coiling even tighter if that were possible.

Helios started his address by thanking everyone for attending, then launched into a witty monologue about his grandfather, which led him neatly into entreating the audience and the hundreds of millions of worldwide viewers to visit the exhibition of the King's life now being held in the palace museum.

And then he cleared his throat.

Amy's own throat closed.

'I would also like to take this opportunity to confirm the speculation about my private life that has been documented in the world's press for these past few weeks. I am honoured to announce that Princess Catalina Fernandez of Monte Cleure has consented to be my wife.'

Such raucous cheers broke out at the news that they drowned out the rest of his speech. The crowd was still whooping when Helios bowed to them all and left the stage, with a grin on his handsome face that looked to Amy's eyes more like a grimace.

Looking around the crowd, blinking to clear the cold fog enveloping her mind, Amy saw that the happiest faces were those of the Agonites who'd been lucky enough to get tickets for this event.

So now it was official.

Helios and the Princess were betrothed. There could be no backing out of the marriage now; not when the pride of two nations was at stake.

And the tiny spark of hope she hadn't even realised she carried in her extinguished into nothing.

Helios shook the hand of yet another post-Gala party guest and silently cursed Talos for disappearing with the violinist, who'd overcome her stage fright and wowed everyone that evening.

His grandfather had retired to bed, exhausted after such a full day, leaving Helios and Theseus to welcome all the people on the three-hundred-strong guest list.

Thank goodness protocol dictated that his fiancée acted in no official capacity until their nuptials had been exchanged. He still couldn't imagine her by his side. Or in his bed.

For the first time he accepted that Amy leaving Agon when he married would be a good thing. The best thing. For all of them.

All he knew was that he wouldn't be able to commit himself to Catalina as a husband if Amy resided under the palace roof and worked in the palace museum.

He'd thought when she had come back to him that everything would be all right and they could return to the way they'd been. But everything was not all right. Everything was worse.

His feelings for her…

There was a trapdoor looming in front of him and every step he made took him closer to falling through it. But he couldn't see in which direction the trapdoor lay. He just knew it was there, readying itself to swallow him whole.

As was normal at a Kalliakis party, none of the guests was in a hurry to leave. But, as was not normal, Helios was in no mood to party with them.

He did his duty and danced with the Princess. Again he felt nothing. His body didn't produce the slightest twinge. Nothing.

When Catalina finally left to catch her flight back to Monte Cleure with her father and brother Helios sought out Theseus, who was still going through the motions with the last of the straggling guests, and bore him away to his apartment.

From the look on his brother's face he needed a drink as much as Helios did.

For someone with a newly discovered son he adored, and a wedding to the boy's mother on the horizon, Theseus was acting like someone who'd been told he was to spend the rest of his life locked in the palace dungeons.

Much as Helios himself felt.

He'd never thought of alcohol as a tool for making problems better—on the contrary, he knew it tended to make matters worse. But he wasn't trying to make himself feel better. That wouldn't be possible. All he wanted was a healthy dose of numbness, even if only for a short time.

Was Amy waiting up for him?

They hadn't made their usual arrangement. It had been on the tip of his tongue to say his customary 'I'll come to you when I'm done' that morning, but this time something had stopped him. A sense of impropriety. Indecency. To parade the news of his fiancée to the world, then expect to slip between the covers with his mistress…

An image flashed into his mind of Amy standing in the cathedral in a wedding dress, of his mother's sapphire ring sliding onto her finger… It was an image he'd been fighting not to see for weeks.

He closed his eyes and breathed deeply.

This was madness.

He took another swig of neat gin and said without thinking, 'Those people watching the Gala. They have no idea of our sacrifices.'

'What?' Theseus slurred, staring at him with bloodshot eyes Helios knew mirrored his own.

'Nothing.'

Even if he'd wanted to confide in his brother,

Theseus was clearly in no state to listen. He knew he should ask him what was wrong, but the truth was he was in no state of mind to listen either.

Moody silence followed, both brothers locked in their own thoughts. The anticipated numbness failed to materialise. All the gin had brought on was the monster of all headaches.

Helios slammed his glass on the table. 'It's time for you to crawl to your own apartment—I'm going to bed.'

Theseus downed his drink without a murmur of protest and got to his unsteady feet. At least his brother was drunk enough to pass out without any problems, he mused darkly.

As Theseus staggered out Helios promised himself that he would leave Amy to sleep. It was long past midnight. Soon the sun would rise. To wake her would be cruel. To go to her at all, tonight of all nights, would be the height of crassness.

Dammit. He'd just become officially engaged. Couldn't he show some decorum for *one* night?

But the memory of Amy's ashen face during the exhibition tour refused to leave him and he knew he had to go to her. He had to see for himself that she was all right.

He walked down the passageway, promising himself that he would leave if there was no answer. When he reached her bedroom door, he rapped on it lightly.

Within seconds he heard the telltale turning of the lock.

When she'd opened the door Amy gazed up at him with an expression he couldn't distinguish. One that combined anguish, desire and need in one big melting pot.

And as he stepped into her welcoming arms he realised that, for all his talk of sacrifice, he didn't yet know how great his biggest sacrifice would be.

With the early-morning sunlight peeking through the curtains, Amy gazed at Helios's sleeping form.

Hours after the post-Gala party had finished he'd come to her. And for the first time since they'd started their relationship all those months ago, nothing physical had happened between them.

Until he'd quietly knocked on her door she'd been trying to sleep, without any luck. She hadn't wanted to stay awake for him. She'd been scared that he wouldn't come to her and equally scared that he would.

Images had tortured her: thoughts of Helios and the Princess dancing together, becoming an official couple, discussing their wedding plans, showing the world how perfect they were for each other. Her stomach had ached so much it had been as if she'd swallowed a jug of battery acid.

With the hours ticking down until morning, she'd assumed the worst. She'd seen the helicopters and limousines taking their honoured guests away from the palace and had been unable to stop herself from wondering which of them carried the Princess.

Then, just as any hope that he would appear had gone, Helios had arrived at her door with bloodshot eyes, exhaustion etched on his face. He'd stripped off his clothes, climbed into her bed, pulled her into his arms and promptly fallen asleep.

How many more nights would he do this? How many more nights would they have together?

The official announcement had set off an alarm clock in her battery-acid-filled stomach and its persistent tick was excruciating.

Careful not to wake him, she sat up, doing nothing but drink him in.

How many more nights could she do this? Simply look at him?

Later that day he would be flying to the US for the start of an official state visit.

In her heart she knew that now, this moment, truly was the beginning of the end for them.

She reached out a hand and gently palmed his cheek. He nuzzled sleepily into her hand and kissed it. Lightly, she began to trace her fingers over the handsome face she loved so much, from his forehead—over which locks of hair had fallen—to his cheekbones, then over the bump on his nose, the bow of his lips, the jawline where thick stubble had broken out, and down his neck. She took his silver chain between her fingers and then touched the mandarin garnet necklace around her own neck.

It had been a birthday present from him, one

he'd given her shortly after they'd started sleeping together. Of all the gifts he'd bestowed upon her, it was the one to which she felt the closest. The meaning behind it, the fact Helios had gone out of his way to find an item of jewellery made with her birthstone, meant that she'd swallowed her guilt and taken it out of the padded envelope where the rest of the jewellery he'd given her remained.

Whatever lay in the future, she knew she would never take it off again.

Slowly she explored his naked body, trailing her fingers over his collarbone and shoulder, down his right arm, lacing them through the fine black hair covering his forearm. When she reached his hand and took each finger in turn, gently pressing into them, he gave a light squeeze in response but otherwise remained still.

After repeating her exploration down his left arm, she moved to his chest. Helios's breathing had changed. It no longer had the deep, rhythmic sound of sleep. A heavier, more ragged sound was coming from him.

Over his pecs she traced her hands, encircling his dark brown nipples, catching the dark hair that was spread finely across his chest, pressing her palm down where the beat of his heart was strongest, then moving them across his ribcage and down to his abdomen…

His erection stopped her in her tracks.

Sucking in a breath, she ignored it, outlining the smooth skin on either side and drawing her fingers over his narrow hips. Gently spreading his muscular thighs, she knelt between them and carried her exploration down his left leg, tracing the silvery scar on his calf—the result of being thrown from a horse at the age of nine—and down to his feet. Then she moved to his right leg, this time starting from his toes and making her way up…all the way to the line where his thigh met his groin.

Helios's hand dug into her hair, spearing it, his breaths now erratic. Still only using her fingers, she traced the long stretch of his erection, cupping him, delighting in his tortured groans, before she put him out of his misery and ran her tongue along its length, then took him into her mouth.

For an age she moved him with her hand whilst licking and sucking. His hand cradled her scalp, massaging it, but he let her set the pace. Heat bubbled deep inside her, burning her from her core outwards, enflaming her skin. Giving him pleasure gave her as much joy as when he pleasured her.

When she sensed him getting close to breaking point she pulled away, unable to give him the playful smile she would normally give. She had never felt less playful when making love to him.

Moving up to straddle him, she gazed into his eyes, thrilling to see the heady desire ringing in them. He cupped her neck and pulled her down to meet his mouth. His tongue swept into hers, his kiss full of all the dark, potent neediness flowing through her own veins.

Slowly, with their lips and tongues still entwined, she sank onto him until he was fully sheathed inside her. Breaking the kiss, she pulled back to sit atop him, needing to look at him.

As his groans became louder he placed one hand flat on her breast, whilst his other hand held tightly to her hip, steadying and supporting her. Then, with her hands resting lightly on his shoulders, she began to move. The feel of him deep inside her, the friction of their movements, it all built on the sensations already whirling inside her.

She could make love to this man every day for the rest of her life and it still wouldn't be enough. She would always want—need—more. Even if they had all the time in the world it wouldn't be enough time for her to look at his face, to touch him, to hear his voice, to witness his smile.

But there was only now, this moment in time when it was just them. There was no palace, no duty...

Just them. One man. One woman.

She wished she could hold on to it for ever.

She tried to hold back the climax growing within her, tried to blunt her responses, but it was all too intoxicating. With a cry that was as much dismay as it was delight, the pulsations swept through her, starting deep in the very heart of her and rippling out to embrace her every atom.

She threw herself down to bury her face in his neck and his arms immediately wrapped around her. A strangled groan escaped his mouth and he gave one last thrust upwards as his own climax tore through him with the same strength as her own. Both of them rode it for as long as they could until there was nothing left but their breaths, burning heavily into each other's necks.

The hotel, arranged by Talia under Helios's instructions, had a charming air to it, an ambience that carried through inside, through the cosy lobby and into the even cosier restaurant.

It was Agon's oldest hotel and a favourite on the tourist trail. It was guaranteed to be busy, whatever the time of year. Thus, two women could meet and dine together during the lunch-time rush without attracting any attention. It was safe for Amy's birth mother here. No one would know who she was. No one would report back to her husband. Ignorance would continue to be bliss for him.

As strange as she knew it to be, Amy would have recognised Neysa even if she hadn't known who she was. Her heart stuttered as she was caught in the gaze of eyes that were identical to her own.

This was the woman who had carried her in her womb for nine months.

This was the woman who had abandoned her.

Neysa Soukis hesitated before asking, 'Amy…?'

'Neysa?' Calling her Mum or Mother was *not* an option.

Grasping the outstretched hand, Amy marvelled at how it was an identical size to her own. It was like seeing a model of herself twenty years from now, although she doubted she would ever be as well groomed. Neysa was expensively dressed and immaculately coiffured.

After ordering drinks and some mezzes Neysa gave a brittle smile, opened her mouth and then closed it again.

Amy filled the silence. 'Why didn't you want to meet me?'

Fingers similar to her own but older, and with buffed nails, drummed on the table. 'You are a stranger to me.' Her English accent was heavy and unpractised.

'You carried me. You gave birth to me.' *You abandoned me.* 'Weren't you curious?'

'I have a life now. Husband. A son.'

Yes… Her son. Leander. The man-child Neysa doted on.

'What made you change your mind?'

She gave a harsh bark of laughter. 'The threat that my husband would learn of you.'

That would be Helios's doing. He was not a man one could say no to. Neysa was here because Helios had effectively blackmailed her, not because she wanted to meet the child she'd given up.

'Leander could tell your husband.'

'Leander would never tell.'

Neysa's confidence in this statement didn't surprise her. Helios had done some more digging into the mother-son relationship and discovered that Leander's father had all but given up on him. Neysa was the one to lavish him with love and the all-important money. He was dependent on her. If she withdrew her funds he would, heaven forbid, have to get a job and keep it.

If her husband was to learn that Neysa had been keeping such a monumental secret from him throughout their twenty-five-year marriage who knew how he would react? Both Neysa and Leander might be thrown off the gravy train they worshipped so much.

A waiter appeared with a tray of drinks.

'Did you ever think of me?' Amy asked when they were alone again.

A flicker of something she couldn't decipher crossed Neysa's face. 'Many times.'

She was lying. Amy didn't know how she could be certain of this, but certain she was. Neysa had forged a new life for herself, with a rich husband two decades her senior. Amy was a dirty little secret she couldn't afford to let anyone find out about. She had no interest in her child. Her only interest was in protecting her secret.

'I knew your father would take good care of you,' Neysa explained earnestly. Too earnestly.

She had known nothing of the sort, and neither had she tried to find out. For all she knew Amy might have been dumped in an orphanage. She'd had no way of knowing that Elaine—the woman who had taken Neysa into her home and trusted her with her young son, the woman Neysa had betrayed in such a heinous way without one word of remorse—had raised Amy as her own.

Amy had spent seventeen years hoping that it had been shame which had kept Neysa away.

That she'd acknowledged that what she'd done to the Green family had been so great a sin that she couldn't bring herself to face Elaine and say sorry.

She couldn't have been more wrong.

At least her father had been genuinely remorseful. Her mum had promised her that. *He'd* acknowledged the terrible deed he'd done and had spent twenty-seven years trying to make amends for it. One mad weekend alone, without his wife and with a hot young woman parading herself around the house before him… He'd been too weak not to take advantage and he'd paid the price every day of his life since.

Looking at her birth mother now, Amy couldn't believe her mum had been able to love her the way she did. Amy was the image of Neysa. Every time her mum had looked at Amy's face she must have seen the image of the woman who had betrayed her and the living proof of her husband's infidelity.

How could Amy even be in the same room as this woman? Neysa hadn't cared that she'd almost destroyed Amy's mum—her *real* mum…

the woman who had loved her every day of her life from the age of two weeks.

And she'd been scared that her mum secretly wanted to get rid of her? Never. Not her loving, generous mum.

The waiter returned to the table with their food.

Amy waited until he'd laid everything out before getting to her feet and hooking the strap of her handbag over her shoulder.

'You have nothing to fear from me,' she said slowly. 'I want no part of your life. I wanted to see you. And now I have.'

'You are going?'

'I shouldn't have come. Goodbye, Neysa.'

Leaving her birth mother open-mouthed in shock, Amy made her way out of the hotel and into the warm spring street brimming with tourists.

She stood for a moment, breathing in the sweet scent. She hadn't found a single place in Agon where the air didn't smell good. And yet an acrid odour lingered around her from her encounter.

Breathing heavily, Amy raised her eyes to the

sky and thanked whatever benevolent being that was up there for allowing Neysa to abandon her.

Who would she be if she'd been raised on Agon under Neysa's narcissistic hand? If she'd grown up with Leander? If she'd lived without Danny and Neil's fierce protection, her mum's loving guidance and her dad's silent but constant presence?

And she thanked Helios too. His interference had allowed her to put to bed one of the biggest questions in her life: who had made her?

That *'who'* was someone she had no wish to see again. But at least she knew that now. Thanks to Helios she could move on and stop wondering *what if...?*

As she thought his name her phone buzzed. It was a brief message from him, checking that everything was okay. Her darling Helios was on a state visit to America and had still found the time to think of her and send her a message.

But how could she be okay? she thought as she replied, saying that she was fine and that she would explain everything to him later, when he called. Which he would. He called her every night when he travelled abroad.

How could everything be okay when very soon she would have to say goodbye to the one person who *did* make everything okay?

CHAPTER ELEVEN

AMY CARRIED ON as best she could over the next few days, never letting her smile drop or her shoulders slouch. She was determined that no one looking at her would have reason to suspect that she was suffering in any way.

The entire island was aflame with gossip following the confirmation of Helios's engagement to the Princess. Naturally this enthusiasm was tripled in the palace itself. Everywhere she went she heard excited chatter. It had got to the stage where, even if she didn't understand what was being said, she imagined it was all about the forthcoming wedding.

The date had been set. In six weeks and one day Helios would marry. It was going to happen sooner than she had thought. She had forgotten about all the work for the wedding that had been going on behind the scenes. Helios had wisely never mentioned it in any of their calls.

Other than in the privacy of her apartment, the only place she found any crumb of solace was amongst the staff in the museum. Whereas the visitors—whose numbers were daily in the thousands—kept up a non-stop commentary about the wedding, the staff took a different approach. They knew Amy had been Helios's lover. *Everyone* had known. So when she was in the same room conversation was kept as far away from matrimony as it was possible to get. But she caught the pitying, often worried glances that were thrown her way.

Her colleagues were a good, kindly, close-knit bunch who supported and looked out for each other. It was in this vein that Claudia, one of the tour guides, approached her in the staff room during Amy's break on the Friday after the Gala.

'I'm sorry to disturb your lunch, but Princess Catalina is here.'

Amy immediately froze, as if a skewer of ice had been thrust into her central nervous system. Somehow she managed to swallow her mouthful of tomato and feta salad, the food clawing its way down her numbed throat.

The tour guide bit her lip. 'She is asking for you.'

'For *me*?' she choked out.

Claudia nodded. 'She wants a tour of the King's exhibition and has asked for you personally.'

It was on the tip of her tongue to ask if Helios was with her, but she stopped herself in time. If Helios was with the Princess they wouldn't need Amy. Helios could do the tour himself.

She didn't even know if he was back from his trip to America. She'd thought he was due back sometime that afternoon.

She'd spent five nights without him.

It had been much harder than any of their other separations. She'd missed him desperately, as a small child missed home.

It was a pain she would have to get used to.

Her main source of comfort had come from Benedict, who had stayed in her apartment during Helios's absence. The lovable black Labrador had seemed to sense Amy's despondency and had kept close to her. Their evenings together had been spent on the sofa, watching films, Benedict's head on her lap.

When she returned to England she would get her own Labrador for company.

Blowing out a long breath of air, Amy closed the lid of her salad box and forced herself to her feet. She couldn't manage another bite.

'Where is she?'

'In the entrance hall.'

'Okay. Give me two minutes to use the bathroom.'

Concentrating on her breathing, Amy took her handbag and locked herself in the staff bathroom. She took stock of her reflection in the mirror and pulled a face. Hastily she loosened her hair from its ponytail, brushed it and then tied it back again. From her handbag she pulled her compressed face powder and a make-up brush and applied a light covering. She would have added eyeliner and lip gloss but her hands were shaking too much.

As a means of buying time for herself, her trip to the bathroom was wasted. The hopes she'd had of making it through the next few months without having to meet the Princess had been blown to pieces.

Why *her*? Why had the Princess asked for her by name? How did she even know who she was?

Terror gripped her, but she forced herself to

straighten up and pushed air into her cramped lungs.

The Princess was an honoured guest, she reminded herself. It was natural she would ask for the exhibition's curator to be her guide. *Just be professional,* she told herself as she left her sanctuary.

The Princess awaited her in the entrance hall, flanked by two huge bodyguards.

She was the epitome of glamour, wearing skintight white jeans, an off-the-shoulder rose-pink top, an elegant pale blue silk scarf and blue high heels. Her ebony hair was loose around her shoulders, and an expensive pair of sunglasses sat atop her head.

But there was more to her than mere glamour; a beautiful, almost ethereal aura she carried effortlessly. She was a princess in every sense of the word. If she slept on a hundred mattresses no doubt she would still feel the pea at the bottom.

Swallowing down the dread lodged like bile in her throat, Amy strode towards her with a welcoming smile. 'Your Highness, I am Amy Green,' she said, dropping into a curtsy. 'It is an honour to meet you.'

The Princess smiled graciously. 'Forgive me for disturbing your break, but I wanted a tour of the exhibition. I've been told you're the curator and that you have a wealth of knowledge about my fiancé's family. I couldn't think of a better person to show me around.' All of this was delivered in almost faultless English.

'I am honoured.' And it *was* an honour. A true honour.

They went slowly around the exhibition rooms, with Amy politely discussing the various artefacts and their context in the Kalliakis family's history. She answered the Princess's questions as best she could whilst all too aware of her constantly clammy hands.

Princess Catalina might look as if she would feel the pea through a hundred mattresses, but she was so much more than a princess from the realms of fairy tales.

She was a flesh and blood human.

It wasn't until they entered The Wedding Room, with the bodyguards keeping a close but respectable distance, that the Princess showed any real animation. She was immediately drawn to Queen Rhea's wedding dress, staring at it adoringly for long, excruciating seconds before she turned to Amy.

'Isn't this the most beautiful dress?' she said with her gaze fixed on her, her eyes searching.

Amy nodded, the bile in her throat burning.

'The dressmaker who made this has agreed to come out of retirement to make mine. I'm having my first fitting tomorrow—did Helios tell you I will be staying at the palace for the weekend?'

'I've heard it mentioned,' she whispered. She'd overheard a couple of the tour guides discussing the visit. They'd been wondering whether the Princess would bring her fabulous Vuitton bag with her. She had.

The Princess smiled. Despite her amiability, sadness lurked behind her eyes. It filled Amy with horror.

'There isn't much that happens within the palace that's kept secret, is there?'

Flames licked her cheeks. It took all her willpower for her not to cover them with her hands.

The Princess seemed not to want a response of the verbal kind. Her sad, probing eyes never left Amy's face, but she smiled. 'I thank you for your time.'

'Do you not want to see the other exhibition rooms?' Caught off guard, Amy took the Princess's hand; a major breach of protocol. She had the softest skin imaginable.

The Princess's squeeze of her hand was gentle and…forgiving? The smile thrown at her was enigmatic. 'I have seen what I came to see.'

Nodding at her bodyguards, she glided away, tall, lithe and poised.

Amy stared at the retreating figure and rubbed the nape of her neck, feeling as if all the wind had been knocked out of her.

The Princess knew.

Dear God, the Princess *knew*.

Her concentration lost, Amy wandered around the exhibition rooms, praying no one would ask her anything that required any thought to answer. Feeling nauseous to the bone, she eventually settled in the entrance hall, trying her hardest to keep herself together.

But all too soon the influx of guests had reduced and reality was given space to taunt her.

The marble sculptures of the four Kings kept

drawing her attention, and as much as she knew she shouldn't she went and stood before them.

King Astraeus the Third had been famed for his wisdom. She wished he could transmute some of it to herself. But it was King Astraeus the Second she couldn't tear her eyes away from. His resemblance to Helios was so strong she could fool herself into thinking it *was* him.

One day, decades from now, a statue much like this would be made of him. If she closed her eyes she could see it, could envisage every inch of the ten-foot marble figure. If the sculptor were to show her the block of stone she would be able to tell him where every line and sinew should go.

It came to her then what she'd been doing that night after the Gala—or early morning—when she'd touched every part of him. She'd been committing him to memory. She hadn't been able to face the truth at the time, but it hit her now. She'd imprinted him on her mind because her subconscious had known that it would be their last time.

Their time together was truly over.

The walls of the great exhibition room suddenly loomed large over her, swallowing her. The statues and the other exhibits blurred. She needed air. But to flee outside would mean risking seeing the Princess or, worse, Helios. She couldn't face him with an audience watching. The next time she saw him she had to be alone with him.

Pulling her identity card from around her neck and stuffing it in her pocket, she walked into the main museum, hurrying through the crowds of visitors until she found Claudia.

'I've got a migraine coming,' she said. 'I need to rest—can you give my apologies to Pedro?'

'Sure.' Claudia looked at her with concern Amy knew she didn't deserve. 'Can I get you anything?'

'No, thank you. Please, I just need to get some sleep in a darkened room.'

Not waiting for a response, Amy wove her way through the remaining people to the private staff entrance to the palace, then hurried up the stairs to her apartment, kicked off her shoes and threw herself onto the bed.

She might not really have a migraine, but her head pounded as if a dozen church bells were ringing inside it. Let it pound. Let the bells clang as loudly as they could and the decibels increase.

She deserved nothing less.

Helios stood in the green stateroom, holding discussions with a group of German business people who wanted to invest considerable sums in Agon's infrastructure and, naturally, recoup their investment with considerable profit. With them was Agon's Transport Minister.

Agon had its own senate, and committees which decided on issues such as outside investors, but an endorsement from one of the royal Princes meant this would be as good as a done deal. Helios knew his opinions carried a great deal of weight and did his utmost to use his influence wisely.

When his phone rang he was tempted to ignore it, but it was his personal phone and only the most important people in his life had been given the number. He frowned when he saw Amy's name on the screen.

He hadn't had a chance to call her and let her know he was back from his trip to the US. In any case he'd assumed she would be busy at the museum… She hardly ever called him and *never* out of the blue.

'Excuse me,' he murmured to the delegation, stepping away from the group with an apologetic smile. He swiped the screen to answer. 'Amy?'

'I'm sorry to disturb you,' she said, her usual soft tones sounding strangely muffled. 'I know you're busy, but I wondered if you're coming to me tonight.'

Not only did she never call him, she never questioned his movements either. A dark sense of foreboding snaked up his spine. 'Is something the matter?'

He heard her hesitation.

'I just need to see you.'

He looked at his watch. 'Where are you?'

'In my apartment.'

'Are you ill?'

'No. Not really. Not ill, ill.'

He wanted to pump her for information but, aware of the delegation, Talia and all the court-iers eyeing him with curiosity, he resisted.

'I'll be with you as soon as I can,' he said, be-fore hanging up.

He'd be with her as soon as he could politely

extricate himself. Something was wrong. The cold dread wedged in the marrow of his bones told him that.

It was half an hour before he was able to extract himself from the group, saying he had some personal business to catch up with and that he would see them at the dinner being held in their honour. He then told Talia that she could leave early. Talia didn't argue the matter—in fact he would swear she left so quickly she left a trail of dust in her wake. He didn't blame her. It had been a long few weeks and she must be exhausted.

When he reached his office he cut through to his apartment and slipped through the passageway into Amy's apartment. She answered his knock quickly, with a startled expression on her face.

'I didn't think I would see you until much later,' she said wanly. 'I hope I haven't put you out.'

'You could never put me out.' He studied her carefully. Her face was grey, her eyes were bloodshot and her hair looked unkempt. 'Have you been crying?'

She bit her lip and took a shuddery breath. Closing the door, she rested her hand on the handle. 'The Princess knows.'

'Catalina? What does she know?'

'About us.' She met his gaze. 'She came to the museum. She wanted me, personally, to give her a tour of the exhibition.'

'You're the exhibition's curator,' he pointed out.

She shook her head. 'It was more than that. She knows, Helios. I think…I think she's heard rumours about us. Maybe someone saw me walking Benedict…I think she was looking for confirmation. Whatever I did, I don't know, but I'm sure something confirmed her suspicions.'

He ran a hand through his hair. 'Even assuming you're right, there is nothing for you to worry about. Catalina isn't stupid. She knows there will be other women.'

It was the wrong thing to say. Amy looked as if he'd slapped her.

'I didn't mean it like that,' he added hastily. 'All I meant was that Catalina has no illusions of fidelity. You know there is no love between us.'

There was nothing between them. Not the smallest twinge.

Shaking her head again, Amy sidestepped past him and went through to her kitchen. 'You're a fool if you believe that. She *wants* it to be a love match.'

'No...'

'Yes,' she said through gritted teeth. 'She does. Whatever you think you know about her, you've got it wrong.'

'She does not love me.'

'Not yet.'

Her eyes bored into his as her words hung in the air between them, then she turned sharply and pulled a bottle of white wine out of the fridge.

'Glass?' she asked.

'You're drinking already?' A trace of his bemusement cut through the darkening atmosphere.

'Right now I need it.'

She leant against the work surface and closed her eyes briefly, then poured them both some wine. When she passed his glass to him she snatched her hand away before there was any chance of their fingers brushing.

She went to take a sip from her own, but as she brought it to her mouth her face crumpled.

Stepping quickly to her, Helios took the glass from her shaking hand and placed it with his own on the counter, then wrapped his arms around her.

At first she resisted, but then she gave in to it, almost burying her head in his chest. Within seconds his shirt was wet with her tears.

'Don't cry, *matakia mou*,' he whispered, stroking her hair. 'It will all work out. I promise.'

'How?' she asked between sobs. 'How can it ever work out? We're breaking her heart.'

'No, we're not.'

'We *are*. Maybe she doesn't love you yet, but she wants to. She wants your marriage to work. Have you even seen her since you got back from America?'

'I've been busy.'

Disentangling herself from his hold, Amy grabbed a handful of tissues from a box. The tears kept falling.

'Helios, the Princess is your fiancée. She's

come all this way to see you. You should be with her. This time before your marriage should be spent getting to know each other...'

'We do know each other.'

'Do you?' She raised her shoulders. 'Then tell me this—what are her dreams? What are her fears? Can you answer any of that? You're going to be spending the rest of your life with her.'

'Yes,' he agreed tightly. 'The rest of my life. But the rest of my life hasn't started yet.'

'It started the minute you put an engagement ring on her finger.'

The engagement ring. He'd told Catalina to choose her own, with the excuse that she would be the one wearing it and so she should have something that was to her own taste. He hadn't been able to bring himself to do the deed himself.

He knew she coveted his mother's sapphire ring. Growing up, he'd always known that ring would be given to the woman he made his wife. He'd had the ready-made excuse that it was a feature of the exhibition to stop him sliding it onto Catalina's finger yet, but he'd promised that when the exhibition was over it would be hers.

'I can't do this any more,' Amy said, her voice choking on the words. 'What we're doing to the Princess is abhorrent. She's a princess but she's *real*, not a fairy-tale creation. She's human, and the guilt is eating me alive.'

He moved to take her back into his arms but she held up a hand to him and shook her head.

'We can't. *I* can't. I won't be the cause of someone else's misery. How can I when I've seen first-hand the damage it causes?' Wiping away a fresh batch of tears, she swallowed before saying, 'When I came to Agon and I wanted to find my birth mother, it wasn't because I wanted to form a relationship with her. I wanted to know my other family and my roots, yes, and I was *desperate* to see what she looked like. But what I really wanted from her was to know why.'

'Why she abandoned you?' She had told him on the phone about the meeting. How she had left within minutes, abandoning the mother who'd abandoned her.

'Partly. What I really wanted to know was how she could have done what she did to my mum. She was her au pair—Mum had trusted her with her child and welcomed her into her home. My mum is the most loving woman in the world. There is no way she would have treated Neysa with anything but kindness. How could she sneak around behind her back with her husband? What kind of evil selfishness makes a person act like that?'

'Did you ask her that?'

'No. I was so desperate to get away from her that I didn't ask her any of the questions I'd been storing up for seventeen years.' She gave a half-hearted shrug. 'And now I don't want to know. I don't want to hear her excuses because that's all they'll be. I don't think she feels any remorse.'

'Amy, our situation is very different. How Neysa and your father behaved...it's not like for like.'

'You might not be married yet, but the intention and commitment are still there. The agony my mum must have gone through... She never got over it. She forgave my father but she's never forgotten, and she's not been able to trust him properly since.'

More tears fell, harder now, turning her face into a torrent of salt water.

'I can't live with the guilt. I've spent my entire life, through no fault of my own, being a person people point at and whisper about. I've had to work so hard to make myself believe that I didn't deserve it and that I was innocent. But how can I be innocent when *I'm* the one now causing someone's misery? I don't want to be the selfish woman Neysa is. I don't want to hurt anyone. The Princess is a good and lovely person and she doesn't deserve this—no one does. Whatever she's been raised to be, she's still human.'

The depth of Amy's guilt and misery stabbed at him, right in his guts, evoking a wave of shame that came rushing through him, a wave so powerful that he reeled and held on to the small kitchen table for support.

'Listen to me,' he said urgently. 'The very fact you feel such guilt proves you are *nothing* like Neysa, so put such thoughts from your mind. You would never hurt anyone, not on purpose.'

'But that is what I've been doing!' she cried. 'I'm *exactly* like her.'

'No! All you inherited from Neysa was her looks. Everything else came from Elaine and the rest of your English family and the goodness that is *you*. You are a good person—the best I know.'

She didn't look the slightest bit convinced by anything he'd said. Helios's mind worked frantically as he tried to think of a solution whereby Amy's guilt could be obliterated. But nothing came to him. He *had* to marry someone of royal blood to secure the Kalliakis line.

He was hurting her, the last thing he'd ever wanted to do. Not Amy. Not her. Not ever.

His father had done more than hurt his mother physically; the destruction had been emotional too. Helios had always known he would never follow his footsteps on the physical side, but to discover he was guilty of an emotional destruction every bit as great...

Something that felt suspiciously like panic clawed at him, biting and contracting through every part of him, converging in his stomach into a pain so acute he wanted to shout out with the agony of it all.

His relationship with Amy was long past being the light, playful interlude it had begun as. Along the way it had developed into something so deep he feared he would no longer be able to see the light if they went any further.

If he had the slightest ounce of decency he would let Amy go before he destroyed her completely.

CHAPTER TWELVE

FOLDING HIS ARMS across his chest, Helios stared at Amy, wondering how he was going to cope without seeing her beautiful face every day and making love to her every night. She was so much more to him than just his lover. She was his best friend, the first true friend he'd ever had. She'd been brought into his life not through her own wealth or social standing but simply by being Amy.

Amy gazed back at him with the same intensity and attempted a brave smile. 'Do you think there's a parallel world out there, where we can be free to be together and love each other?'

Love?

She must have registered the shock in his eyes at her use of the *L* word for she laughed wanly. 'Oh, I do love you. Very much. More than I ever knew was possible.'

He stepped out of her reach, backing himself

against the kitchen door. He didn't know how to answer. He couldn't think.

His private phone buzzed in his pocket. He pulled it out and rejected the call without looking at it.

'Love is not something I have ever required,' he finally said, his brain reeling as much as his body.

'I know that.' Her chin wobbled and she took deep breaths, raising her eyes to the ceiling.

'*Theos*, Amy, you...' He blew out a long breath as his brain scrambled to unravel itself. 'I've always known I must marry for duty. Love isn't something I've ever expected or thought about. It has no place in my life, you must see that?'

'Yes, I do.'

Of course she did. Amy knew his full ancestral history better than she could ever know her own.

'If you love me then how can you leave me?' he asked, still shell-shocked at her declaration but grasping at straws.

'Because I want to be able to look at my reflection every day and not throw darts at it,' she answered with a choked laugh. 'And my leaving isn't just to do with Catalina.'

There. She'd finally uttered the Princess's name aloud.

'I might have been made from a dirty secret but I don't want to live my life as one. You're right that I'm not Neysa, and I will not allow myself to be like her. Even if you wanted it— even if you loved me—you're not in a position to give me the commitment and fidelity I need. I want to be yours. Just yours. Openly yours. With the whole world knowing we belong together. I can't make love with you while you're sleeping in the bed of another, and I can't make love knowing I'm good enough for sex but not good enough for for ever.'

What she didn't say was that Helios had lodged himself so deeply into her heart she doubted there was room left in there for any other man to find an opening. Her heart belonged to him now.

She should have left weeks ago. The physical pain she'd experienced when he'd told her of his intention to marry as soon as possible should have acted as a warning. If she'd gone then she would have left with her pride intact and her heart would still have enough room for someone else.

His face contorted. 'Don't you *ever* say you're not good enough.'

'But that's how I feel,' she said, shrugging her shoulders helplessly. 'I know that's not your intention, and that you don't think or believe that—I *know*—but I've spent most of my life feeling like a dirty secret. For us to carry on, even if it's only until you marry, will *make* me one.'

He didn't say anything, just stared at her as if he were seeing her for the first time.

'Helios, when you marry the Princess be faithful to her. Give your marriage a chance. She deserves that and so do you.'

'You sound like you're planning to leave now...' A strange look flashed in his eyes and suddenly he sprang to life like *Galatea*, the statue created with such love by Pygmalion.

He strode out of the kitchen and into her bedroom, taking in the suitcases on the bed, half-filled with clothing.

His face contorted and he shook his head. 'No.'

'Helios...'

'No.' His hands clenched into fists.

She could see him fighting the urge to throw her cases out of the window.

His phone buzzed again, the third time it had rung in as many minutes.

'Answer it,' she insisted. 'It might be important.'

'*This* is important.' After a moment's pause he swore and pulled the phone to his ear. 'Yes?'

After a few moments his demeanour changed. As he listened he straightened his neck and rolled his shoulders, breathing deeply. His only contribution to the conversation was a few short words of Greek.

'I need to go,' he said when he'd finished the call. 'My grandfather's suffering from a mild infection and is fighting with the doctors over his treatment.'

'I hope it's nothing too serious,' she said, immediately concerned.

'Just my grandfather being a stubborn old man.' He rubbed his chin and glared at her with his jaw clenched. 'I'll be back later. Don't even *think* of going anywhere.'

She didn't answer.

'I need to hear it, Amy. Tell me you won't go anywhere or do anything until I get back. Promise me.'

Knowing even as she spoke them that her words were a lie, she said, 'I'll be here.'

His shoulders loosened a little. Pacing over to her, he took her face in his hands and crushed her lips with his mouth, kissing her as if he'd been starved of her kisses for ever. And then he dropped his hold on her and walked out of her bedroom.

She heard the slam of the interconnecting door as he left.

Theos, his grandfather had to be the most stubborn man alive. He was refusing the intravenous drugs his doctors wanted to give him.

What could he do? He couldn't force him. The King wasn't a baby to be coaxed into doing his elders' bidding.

That hadn't stopped Helios from trying to make him see reason. Now he wanted to tear his hair out, to claw at his scalp and draw blood.

'At least he's not in pain,' Talos said quietly.

Their grandfather hadn't resisted painkillers for the pain racking his body. The cancer, kept at bay by months of chemotherapy, was making another, deadlier assault on his body. No one would say it, but time was slipping away from them.

One good thing to come out of the mess this day had turned into was the news from Theseus, who had gone tearing after Jo, the mother of his child, a couple of days ago. The fool had realised when it was almost too late that he truly did love her, and luckily it seemed Jo loved him too and had agreed to marry him.

No coercion, no thoughts of duty. They were marrying for love. Helios had never heard his brother sound so happy.

Both his brothers were marrying.

As Talos—who was marrying his violinist— had chosen someone not of royal blood, any child he had would not be in the line of succession to the throne, but Toby, Theseus's beautiful son, had already secured the throne for the next generation. Until Helios's own children were born.

Helios sighed and got to his feet. 'I need to change for dinner.'

He wished he could pull out of it, but it was a matter of honour amongst his family that personal matters never got in the way of duty. And this dinner was duty.

Nausea fermented in him as he remembered that Catalina would be attending. She was already there in the palace. He still couldn't bring himself to call her.

As much as he wanted to, there wasn't time to make a diversion to Amy's apartment and check that she was okay. Instead he fired off a quick message to her before showering and changing into his dinner jacket. He put his cufflinks on during his walk to the designated dining room for the evening, his courtiers struggling to keep up with his long strides.

Forcing bonhomie, Helios plastered a smile on his face and entered the dining room, where the delegation was waiting for him. Catalina was already there, holding court like a professional. When she saw him she excused herself to join him.

If she really did suspect him and his relationship with Amy, she covered it well.

'I understand your grandfather is unwell?' she said quietly.

'He's been better.' It was all he could bring himself to answer with.

Why couldn't he feel anything for her? Here was

a beautiful, compassionate woman of royal blood and all he felt when she touched him was cold.

He tried again, using a milder tone of voice. 'He has an infection.'

She smiled sympathetically. 'I hope he recovers quickly.'

'So do I.'

But he didn't hold out much hope. These past five months had been a battle to keep him alive long enough for him to see the Gala. That was all his grandfather had been focusing on. Now, with the Gala over, his grandsons all paired off and the succession to the throne secured, King Astraeus was preparing to die.

His duty was done. His grandfather wanted to be with the woman he'd loved for his entire adult life.

And Amy had said she loved *him*.

Helios wished he could unhear those words.

What kind of selfish monster was he to tie her to him when he knew doing so was destroying her?

It was possibly the longest meal of his life. For once, the power of speech had deserted him. He couldn't think of a single witty remark or any of the tales that usually had guests enthralled.

Throughout the meal disquiet grew within him, a foreboding which came upon him from an unseen direction.

As soon as the coffee had been cleared away he cleared his throat. 'My apologies, ladies and gentlemen, but I need to retire for the evening. I know I haven't been very good company this evening—I think exhaustion has crept up on me—but be assured that I am very impressed with everything you've told me and will give my recommendation to the committee early next week.'

When he'd finished speaking he glanced at Catalina. She was staring at him with a cool, thoughtful expression.

It took fifteen minutes, time spent saying goodnight to everyone individually, before he was finally able to leave the dining room.

Catalina made no effort to follow him.

The disquiet in his chest grew with every step he took towards his apartment. By the time he reached his door and was able to shake off the courtiers, perspiration had broken out on his brow and his pulse had surged.

He headed straight down the passageway and rapped on Amy's connecting door.

No answer.

He banged again, louder.

No answer.

'Amy?' he shouted, pounding on the door with his fist.

On impulse he tried the handle, even though Amy always kept the door locked…

The door opened.

His heart thundering painfully beneath his ribs, he stepped into her apartment.

'Amy?' he called into the silence.

His heart knew before his head could comprehend it.

On legs weighted down with lead, he stepped into her bedroom.

The room was spotless. And empty.

All that lay on the dressing table, which was usually heaped with cosmetics and bottles of perfume, was a large padded envelope he recognised as the one he'd given to her all those weeks ago, containing the jewellery he'd bought her. Next to it lay a scrap of paper. Written on it were two words.

Forgive me.

* * *

'You look troubled, Helios,' his grandfather said, in the wheezing voice Helios hated so much.

They were playing chess, his grandfather's favourite game. The King was in his wheelchair, an oxygen tank to his right, a nurse set back a little to his left.

'I'm just tired.' Helios moved a pawn two spaces forward, unable to stop his stomach curdling with the fear that this might be the last game they played together.

'How are the wedding preparations going?'

'Well.'

Not that he was having anything to do with them. The palace staff were more than capable of handling it without his input. And without Catalina, who seemingly had as much interest in the preparations as he had. None at all.

His grandfather placed the oxygen mask on his face for a minute, before indicating for the nurse to take it off.

'I remember my own wedding day well.' The misty eyes grew mistier. 'Your grandmother looked like an angel sent from heaven.' Then the old eyes sharpened. 'Your mother looked beautiful on her wedding day too. It is my eternal sorrow that your father couldn't see her beauty. Your mother was beautiful, inside and out.'

Helios's spine stiffened. His parents' marriage was a subject they rarely touched upon other than in the most generic terms.

'The biggest regret of my life—and your grandmother's, rest her soul—was that your father couldn't choose his own wife. Would it have made a difference if he'd been able to choose?' He raised a weak, bony shoulder. 'We will never know. Despite our best efforts he was a vain and cruel man. He thrived on power. Your mother didn't stand a chance.'

He moved his castle forward with a quivering, gnarled finger.

'We pushed through the changes in law that would allow you and your heirs to select your own spouses in the hope that your parents' marriage would never be repeated.' His voice weakening with each word he said, the King turned his gaze to Helios again. 'However important duty is, marriage to someone you feel no affection for can only bring misery. And for ever is a long time to be miserable.'

The nurse, attuned to his weakening, placed the oxygen mask back over his face.

Helios waited for him to inhale as much as he needed, all the time his mind was reeling over what it was, exactly, that his grandfather was trying to tell him. Was it a reproach that he wasn't spending enough time with Catalina and that his indifference to her was showing?

But how could he feel anything *but* indifference when his head was still consumed with thoughts of Amy? She'd left the palace a week ago but she was still *everywhere*.

He moved his knight, then opened his mouth to pose the question, only to find his grandfather's head had lolled to one side and he'd dozed off mid-game and mid-conversation.

He looked at the nurse, who raised her shoulders sympathetically. Helios exhaled and gazed at his sleeping grandfather, a huge wave of love washing through him.

Whatever his grandfather had tried to tell him, it could wait.

'I'll put him to bed tonight,' he told the nurse, whose eyes immediately widened in fright.

'It's okay,' he assured her with a wry smile.

'I know what I'm doing. You can supervise if you want.'

Half an hour later the King was in his bed, his medication having been given and the oxygen mask attached to his face. His gentle snores were strangely calming.

Helios placed a kiss to his grandfather's forehead. 'I love you,' he said, before leaving him to sleep.

Movement beside her woke Amy from the light doze she'd fallen into. Since returning to England a week ago she'd slept a lot. She liked sleeping. It was the perfect route to forgetting. It was waking that was the problem.

Her mum handed her a cup of tea and sat in the deckchair next to her.

When she'd returned to England she'd given the taxi driver directions to her childhood home rather than the flat she shared in central London. Sometimes a girl just needed her mum. Her *real* mum. The woman who'd loved and raised her since she'd barely been able to open her eyes.

And her mum had been overjoyed to see her.

Amy's last lingering doubts had been well and truly banished.

A late-night confession between them had culminated with the admission that her mum had been terrified that Amy would forge a relationship with Neysa.

'Never,' Amy had said with a firm shake of her head. 'You're my mum. Not her.'

'Good.' Ferocity had suddenly flashed in her mum's usually calm eyes. 'Because you're *my* daughter. Not hers.'

'Then why did you encourage me to learn about my roots?' she'd asked, bewildered.

'We all need to know where we come from. And I was scared that if I discouraged it you would do it in secret and one day you'd be gone and I would lose you.'

'You will never lose me.'

The tears had flowed easily that night.

Now they sat in companionable silence in the English sun, the only sound the chirruping of fledgling birds in the garden's thick hedges. It was a quintessentially British beautiful late-spring day.

'Are you ready to talk now?' her mum asked.

A lump forming in her throat, Amy shook her head. For all their late-night talks, she hadn't been able to bring up the subject of Helios.

To even think of him was too painful.

She'd had only one piece of correspondence from him since she'd left—a text message that said: I do.

He forgave her for running away.

Judging by his silence since, he'd accepted it too. She had no right to feel hurt that he'd made no further attempt to contact her.

'What's that you keep fingering around your neck?'

Wordlessly, Amy leaned forward to show her the garnet necklace.

Her mum took it between her fingers and smiled. 'It's lovely.'

Amy couldn't find the words to answer. When her mum let the necklace go Amy clasped it in her own hand and held it close.

'Broken hearts do mend,' her mum said softly.

Amy gave a ragged nod and swallowed, terrified of crying again. 'It hurts,' she choked out.

Her mum took her hand and squeezed it. 'Do you know what to do when life gives you lemons?'

'Make lemonade?'

'No. You throw them back and get yourself an orange.'

Amy spluttered, laughing. 'I haven't the faintest idea what that means.'

'Neither do I! It was something my mother used to say when I was a child.'

Still holding on tightly to each other's hands, they settled back in their deckchairs, sunglasses on, and basked in the sun.

After a while, her mum spoke again. 'I think what my mother was trying to say is that, whatever life throws at you, there are always choices and options other than the obvious ones. When your father first brought you home the obvious solution for me would have been to throw him out, and you with him. That would have been me making lemonade. But when I looked at you all I saw was an innocent, helpless newborn baby— a sister to the child I already had and a sister to the child I carried in my belly. So I chose to get myself an orange instead. I kept you—*you* were my orange. And I have never regretted it. My only regret is that I never carried you in my womb like I did your brothers.'

She took her sunglasses off and smiled the warm, motherly smile Amy loved so much.

'This man who's broken your heart…is he a good man?'

'He's the best,' she whispered.

'Is he worth the pain?'

She jerked a nod.

'Then you have to decide whether you're going to make lemonade or find an orange. Are you going to wallow in your pain or turn it into something constructive?'

'I wouldn't know where to start.'

'You start by accepting the pain for what it is but refusing to let it define you.'

Amy closed her eyes. If anyone knew how to cope with pain it was her mum. She'd handled a mountain of it and had never let it define her.

Compared to her mum she had nothing to complain about. Her mum had been innocent. She, Amy, had brought her misery upon herself.

Helios stood at the door to his grandfather's apartments and braced himself for the medicinal odour that would attack his senses when he stepped over the threshold.

Inside, all was quiet.

Stepping through to what had once been the King's bedroom and now resembled a hospital ward, he found his grandfather sleeping in his adjustable medical bed, with an oxygen mask over his nose and mouth.

At his side sat Helios's brothers. A nurse read unobtrusively in the corner.

'Any change?' he asked quietly. He'd only left the room for an hour, but the speed of his grandfather's deterioration over the past couple of days had been frightening. They all knew it wouldn't be long now.

Talos shook his head.

Taking his place on the other side of the bed from his brothers, Helios rolled his shoulders. Every part of his body felt stiff.

Theseus was holding their grandfather's right hand. Leaning forward, Helios took the left one, assuming the same position his grandfather had taken when his Queen had lain in an identical bed in the adjoining room, the life leaching out of her.

After a few long, long minutes their grandfather's eyes fluttered open. 'Water...' he croaked.

With Helios and Theseus working together from separate sides of the bed to raise him, Talos brought a glass to his mouth and placed the straw between his lips.

When he'd settled back the King looked at his three grandsons, his stare lingering on each of them in turn, emotion ringing the rapidly dulling eyes.

The pauses between each of his inhalations grew. Then the corners of his lips twitched as if in a smile and his eyes closed for the last time.

CHAPTER THIRTEEN

AMY SAW THE announcement on the morning news.

'A statement from the palace said, "His Majesty King Astraeus the Fourth of Agon passed away peacefully in his sleep last night. His three grandsons were at his side.'"

There then followed some speculation by the presenters and royal correspondents about what this meant for the island nation.

Without warning a picture of Helios and Catalina flashed onto the screen. It was an unofficial shot taken at the Gala. And then there was an off-screen voice saying, 'It is believed the heir to the throne will marry the Princess before taking the crown.'

Amy switched off the television, grabbed a pillow and cuddled into it, her head pounding.

Helios's grandfather, the King, had *died*.

She'd known it was coming, but still it hit her

like a blow. She'd created his exhibition. During those happy months of curating that tribute to his life and the ancestors closest to him she'd felt as if she'd got to know him. Somehow she'd fooled herself into believing he was immortal. He had been a proud, dutiful man and she'd been privileged to meet him.

And then she thought of his eldest grandson, who had revered him.

Her phone lay on the floor beside her and she stared at it, wishing with all her heart that she could call Helios.

Would he even want to hear her condolences? The condolences of the woman who had sneaked out of the palace while he was dining with potential investors, supporting the island he loved?

She'd told him she would stay.

He'd forgiven her lie, but he had Catalina now. Without Amy's presence there, distracting him, he would turn to the Princess for comfort. Just as he should. Maybe grief would bring them together properly.

And as she prayed for a happy ending for her Prince and his Princess, hot tears spilled out of her eyes. She brought her knees to her chest and cried her broken heart out for the happy ending that would never be hers.

The funeral, a full state affair, was a sombre occasion.

People lined the streets in tens of thousands, all there to bow their heads in silence and pay their respects to the man who had served them with such dedication for fifty years.

The wake was an entirely different matter.

Out on the streets the atmosphere changed markedly. Television coverage showed military re-enactments from throughout the ages, even children dressed in loincloths and armed with plastic tridents. Barbecues lit up Agon's famous beaches, music played on every corner and there was food, drink and dancing everywhere in abundance.

Agon was putting on a show in the only way it knew how.

In the blue stateroom of the palace solemnity had given way to merriness too. The King was with his Queen. His suffering was over. His country and his family had laid him to rest and now they could celebrate his life.

For Helios, the occasion brought no joy. He accepted that his grandfather had moved on to a better place, but the hole in his heart felt so great he didn't know how it would ever heal.

To know he would never talk to him again, dine with him, play chess… All the things he'd taken for granted were all gone. The man he'd worshipped, a man ten times the man his own father had been, was gone.

Helios watched his brothers, stuck like glue to the sides of their respective fiancées, and smiled for them. Their parents' marriage had been the worst template a child could have asked for. That his brothers were heading into marriages that would be more like their grandparents' gave him much hope. They would be happy.

He was under no illusions that he would follow suit.

Although he had seen little of her since his grandfather's death, Catalina had been at his side throughout the funeral service, a calm presence who had known exactly what to say in all the right moments.

But, however perfect she might be, he knew that fifty years of marriage wouldn't bring them the bond Talos and Theseus shared with their fiancées.

That last smile his grandfather had given them was a white shadow in Helios's mind. It gave him comfort. His grandfather had welcomed death. He'd left the world knowing his grandsons—all of them—would take care of his beloved island, freeing him to move on to his beloved Rhea.

His *three* grandsons.

Three boys raised to be princes.

Catalina came to stand by him. He stared down at her and met her thoughtful gaze.

'Marriage to someone you feel no affection for can only bring misery.'

Those were the words his grandfather had said the last time they'd spoken lucidly together. And in that moment he knew those words hadn't been a reproach. They'd been a warning from a man who knew how powerful love could be and had witnessed the destructive nature of his son's contempt for the wife he didn't love.

And in that instant everything became clear.

He couldn't marry Catalina.

If he'd never met Amy everything would be different. *He* would be different.

If he'd never met Amy he would be marrying Catalina with no expectations or knowledge of how things might be. He would be King. She would be Queen. Their only bond would be of duty. He wouldn't know what it felt like to love or be loved.

Love.

The one word he'd never expected to apply to himself other than in an abstract form. Familial love he'd felt and believed in, but romantic love…? That was not something he'd ever been able to hope for, so not something he had ever allowed himself to think about. And, if he was being honest with himself, it was something he'd hidden away from. The scars of his parents' marriage ran so deep that what he'd convinced himself was rational acceptance of his future union was in fact a mask to hide the real truth— that love in all its forms was the most terrifying emotion of all.

But also the most wonderful.

Because, *Theos*, he loved Amy. With everything he had.

Try as he might, he couldn't get used to walking into the museum and not seeing her there.

He couldn't get used to being in his apartment and seeing the connecting door, knowing she wasn't at the end of the passageway.

Not a second of his waking day was spent without him wondering where she was and what she was doing.

After his grandfather's death had been announced he'd kept staring at his phone, willing it to ring. Knowing it wouldn't. Knowing she was right not to call him.

But his intellectual acceptance that she was gone and that it was all for the best wasn't something his heart had any intention of agreeing with.

He'd long trusted Amy with his confidences. Now he understood that he'd also trusted her with his heart, and that a relationship with any other woman was doomed to failure because he belonged to Amy. All of him.

When the day of his own death came the last thing his conscious mind would see would be her face.

Three weeks without her.

The time had dragged like a decade.

How could he think straight without her?

How could he breathe without her when she was as necessary to him as air?

He loved her.

He cast his eyes around the room until he found Theseus, deep in conversation with his fiancée, Jo, and a Swedish politician the three Princes had been at school with. Theseus was settled. He had a child. His marriage would be taking place in a week.

Helios took a deep breath. Before he spoke to his brother there was someone else who needed to be spoken to first.

He looked at her, still by his side, the silence between them stark.

'Catalina...'

'We need to talk, don't we?' she said quietly.

'Yes.'

Weaving their way through the crowd, they walked through a corridor, and then another, and then stepped out into the palace gardens.

'Catalina, I'm sorry but I can't marry you.'

She closed her eyes and breathed deeply.

'I've been grossly unfair to you. I'm not...' It was his turn to take a breath. 'I'm in love with someone else.'

She bowed her head and eventually met his gaze. 'Thank you for finally being honest with me—and with yourself.'

'I never meant to hurt you.'

Her smile was stoical. 'All you have hurt is my pride.'

He opened his mouth to speak further but she raised a hand to stop him.

'It would never have worked between us. I've known it for a while now, but I didn't want to add to the burden you've carried with your grandfather's illness.' She sighed. 'I will get my people to issue a press release in a couple of days, saying I have called the engagement off due to an incompatibility between us.'

It was the least he could let her do. 'Catalina, I am sorry. I never wanted...'

'No. Do not say anything else.' She lifted her chin. 'Let me leave here with *some* dignity.'

For a moment Helios did nothing but stare at the woman he had intended to spend the rest of his life with. Then, taking her shoulders, he pulled her into his embrace. It warmed his heart to feel her arms wrap around his waist.

'You will find a better man than me,' he whispered.

'I doubt that,' she answered drily. 'But perhaps I will find a man whose heart is free to love me.'

'I hope that for you too.'

Pulling apart, they kissed each other on both cheeks and smiled.

The weight he carried on his shoulders lifted a fraction.

'I expect an invitation,' she said as she walked away.

'An invitation to what?'

'To your wedding to your English curator. Your mother's ring will look wonderful on her finger.'

With one final wink she sashayed into the palace, not looking back.

Alone in the gardens Helios did a slow turn, taking in the verdant lawns, the sweet-scented flowers in bloom, the distant maze. It was a paradise of nature and life. Whether he became custodian of it all, as he'd spent his entire life believing he would, or not, the flowers would continue to bloom. That he knew with absolute certainty.

His heart beating loudly, echoing through every chamber of his body, he took his phone out of his pocket and dialled the number he had spent the past three weeks fighting not to call.

It went straight to voicemail.

He tried again.

The same thing happened.

Back in the palace, he entered the stateroom and found the person he was looking for.

'I need to borrow you,' he said to Pedro, interrupting his Head of Museum's conversation with a person he did not recognise.

'Where are we going?' Pedro asked.

'To the museum. I need to get something.'

The museum was closed out of respect for his grandfather and to allow all the staff to pay their respects too.

With long strides they followed the corridors into the museum's private entrance and cut through the large exhibition rooms until they reached the rooms that mattered to Helios at that moment. The Kalliakis Family exhibition rooms.

After he'd explained to Pedro what he wanted, a thought struck him.

'Do you know where Amy's working now?'

'She's back at the British Museum.'

No wonder she'd turned her phone off. She would be working. 'Do you have the number?'

Pedro scrolled through his phone until he found the relevant number and thrust the phone at him.

Helios put it to his ear whilst indicating that Pedro could start on the task he'd set for him. It rang a couple of times, a passage of time that to Helios's ears was longer than for ever, before it was answered.

'Put me through to Amy Green,' he said.

'One moment, please.'

There followed a merry little game in which he was routed to varying offices until a voice said, 'Ancient Greece Department.'

'I wish to speak to Amy Green.'

'I'm sorry, sir, but Amy is on leave. She'll be back on Monday.'

'Do you know where she's gone?'

'As far as I'm aware she's attending a funeral.'

'Thank you.'

Disconnecting the call, his brain reeling, Helios rubbed the nape of his neck.

Now what?

And as he wondered what the hell his next step should be his heart went out to her. To think she too had lost someone important… She would be in need of comfort just as he—

And in the space of a heartbeat he knew whose funeral she'd attended.

Hope filled him, spreading from his toes right to the roots of his hair.

He put a call through to his private secretary. 'Talia,' he said as soon as she answered, 'I need you to find Amy Green for me. She's in the country. Go through to Immigration and take it from there.'

To her credit, Talia took his instructions in her stride. 'The Immigration Minister is here.'

'Good. Speak to him. Now.'

While all this was going on Pedro had completed the task he'd been set and so the pair of them reset the alarms, closed the museum and went back to the wake.

Helios found Talia in a quiet corridor, with her phone pressed to her ear by her shoulder, writing information on her hand. She gave him a thumbs-up and carried on her conversation.

'She's at the airport,' she said without preamble a few minutes later. 'Her flight back to England leaves in forty-five minutes. The passengers for her flight will be boarding any minute.'

'I need to get to the airport.'

A tremor of fear flashed over Talia's face. 'All the roads are blocked. You'll never make it in time.'

'Watch me.'

With that, he headed back into the stateroom and, ignoring everyone who tried to speak to him, found the butler of Theseus's private villa, Philippe, a man who looked as if he should be catching the surf, not running a Prince's household.

He pulled him aside to speak to him privately.

'You have a motorbike, don't you?'

'Yes, Your Highness.'

'Is it here at the palace?'

'It's in the staff courtyard.'

'I need to borrow it.'

'Now?'

'Now.'

'Do you know how to ride?'

'You have the time it takes us to walk there to teach me. Let's go.'

* * *

Amy stared out of the oval window with a heavy heart.

She was glad she'd come.

It had been a snap decision, driven by a sense of certainty that she had to go, to pay her respects to the man for whom she'd devoted almost six months of her life to creating an exhibition of *his* life.

Watching Helios and his brothers walking with military precision in front of the coffin, their gazes aimed forward, knowing how they must be bleeding inside...

The crowds had been so thick there had been no chance of Helios catching sight of her, but even so she hadn't taken any chances, keeping a good distance from the barrier.

What good would it have done for him to see her? The Princess had been there for him, just as Amy had known she would be, travelling in an official car with Theseus's and Talos's fiancées.

A steward made his sweep down the aisle, checking everyone's seat belts were fastened. The plane began to move. Over the speakers came the sombre voice of the captain, welcoming them all to this flight to London.

The ache in her chest told her she'd been wise to get a return flight home straight after the funeral. Any longer and the temptation to call Helios and seek him out would have become too great to resist. One night on Agon was as much as she'd been prepared to risk.

She'd taken her mother's advice to heart, and God knew she was trying to get herself an orange.

She'd taken up her old job at the museum and enrolled in a postgraduate course on the Ancient Romans, which she would start in September. She figured she might as well expand her knowledge so that her life wasn't all about Agon and its people, whether from history or the present. There was a big world out there to explore and learn about.

She'd kept herself busy, working by day and socialising by evening. It was the nights that were unbearable. Despite the mild heatwave sweeping through the UK, her nights were always cold.

Somehow she would find a way to forget him.

The plane had reached the place where it would turn around and face the runway.

The woman sitting beside her gripped the arm-rests, her knuckles turning white in anticipation of take-off.

But no sooner had the plane started its journey down the runway than it was brought to a stop.

It took a while before the passengers realised something was wrong, and then low murmurs began spreading throughout the plane.

The voice of a stewardesses came over the speaker. 'Could passenger Miss Amy Green please make herself known to a member of the cabin crew?'

Amy barely heard, her attention caught by a motorcyclist, speeding over the tarmac, heading towards them. Behind him was a buggy, with two men in orange high-visibility jackets towing metal steps. There was something about the figure riding the motorbike…

'Amy Green? Miss Amy Green—please make yourself known to a member of the cabin crew.'

With a jolt she realised it was *her* they were asking for. Tearing her gaze away from the window, she raised a hesitant hand.

A stewardess bustled over to her, looking harassed. 'Amy Green?'

Amy nodded, bemused and not a little scared.

'I need you to come with me.'

'Why?'

'We've been asked to escort you off this flight.'

'But *why*? Have I done something wrong?'

The stewardess shook her head. 'I don't know why.'

The couple she was sitting next to had to get out of their seats to let her pass, but it wasn't long before she was trailing the stewardess to the exit, her face burning with mortification, her brain burning with confusion.

What the hell was going on...?

At the rear exit of the plane the crew were all staring at her unabashedly, no doubt wondering if she was some kind of fugitive.

Was she a fugitive? Had she unwittingly committed a crime that necessitated her being escorted off a plane and arrested?

And then the door opened, the metal stairs were hastily bolted on and she stood at the threshold, looking to see if a dozen police officers were waiting at the bottom to take her into custody.

The only person waiting for her was the motorcyclist she'd spotted. He sat astride the bike, his helmet resting under an arm…

CHAPTER FOURTEEN

Amy's heart leapt so hard it almost jumped out of her mouth.

Behind her came a collective sigh from the crew. One of them squeezed her shoulder. 'Go to him.'

But she couldn't. Her legs had turned to jelly.

She covered her mouth, unable to believe her eyes.

What was he doing here?

His handsome face immobile, he got off his bike, placed the helmet on the seat and climbed the stairs with heavy treads.

It was only when he was at eye level with her and she was able to gaze into the liquid dark brown eyes she loved so much that Amy dared to breathe.

'Helios,' she whispered, raising a hand to brush it against his cheek, to feel for herself that he truly was there and that this wasn't some dream she'd fallen into.

But no. No dream.

His cheek was warm and smooth, his jawline rough, at the stage where stubble was just starting to poke through the skin. His warm, familiar scent played under her nose.

'Sneaking away again?' he asked, in a voice that was meant to be humorous but that cracked on the last syllable.

'What…? What are you doing here?'

His eyes bored into her, emotion seeping out of them. 'I'm taking you home.' Then he took the final step up and lifted her into his arms. 'I'm taking you home,' he repeated.

Another collective 'Ooh…' sounded from behind her, and as Helios carried her down the steps a round of applause broke out. One of the men in high-visibility jackets, who was waiting by the buggy, wolf-whistled.

Amy heard it all, but none of it penetrated. All her senses were focused so intensely on her lover that everything else had become a blur.

At the bottom of the steps Helios placed her carefully on her feet.

Suddenly the biggest, widest grin spread over his face. 'Would Despinis Green like a ride on my bike?'

Laughter bubbled up in her throat and broke through her daze. She flung her arms around him. 'Yes. Please. Take me anywhere.'

Amy kept a tight hold on Helios as he drove them through the streets of Resina. She didn't *have* to hold him tightly—the dense throng of partying people meant he had to ride at a snail's pace—but she needed to. Keeping her cheek pressed into the solidity of his back and her arms around his waist grounded her, helped her accept the reality of what had just happened.

Soon they had passed through the capital and were out in the verdant countryside, with Agon's mountains looming before them. Helios found a road that took them up Mount Ares, the rockiest of Agon's mountains, past goats casually chewing grass by sheer drops, taking them higher and higher until they arrived at a clearing.

He turned the engine off and clicked the stand down to keep the bike upright before helping her off.

She looked at him, laughing as she properly noticed for the first time that he'd ridden with her up a mountain in a pair of handmade black trousers, black brogues, now covered in dust, and a white shirt with the sleeves rolled up that had probably been as crisp as freshly baked pie earlier but was now crumpled and stained.

'Your clothes are ruined.'

He shrugged, his eyes sparkling. 'I couldn't care less.'

Taking her hand, he led her to a flat grassy area and sat down, enfolding her in his arms so her back rested against his chest and her head was tucked beneath his chin.

'When I was a child my brothers and I would race to the top of this mountain. When we'd all reached the summit we would come down to this clearing and eat our picnic. This spot has the best view of the sunset on the whole of Agon.'

The sun was already making its descent, causing a darkly colourful hue to settle over the island.

'How did you know I was here?' she asked eventually.

'Your museum told me you'd gone to a funeral. I guessed.'

'But how did you know what plane I was on?'

'Do you really need me to answer that?' he said with bemusement.

She smiled to herself, tightening her hold on his hands, which were still wrapped around her waist. And then she remembered *why* she had come to Agon today.

'I'm so sorry about your grandfather,' she said softly.

He kissed her head. 'He was ready to go.'

'I wanted to call you.'

'I know you did. And you were right not to.'

She sighed. Now that she had come to her senses, reality was poking at her painfully.

'How did you manage to sneak out without your bodyguards?'

'Simple. I didn't tell them what I was doing. The palace was so busy with the wake it was easy. Talia will have told them by now.'

'She knows you came for me?'

'Yes. So does Pedro.'

'How long do we have? Here, I mean?'

'As long as we want.'

'But you'll be missed,' she said with another sigh, thinking that, however wonderful it was to be sat in his arms again, she would be dragged away from him again soon.

She was here now, though. A short interlude. Two lovers snatching a few minutes together to watch the sunset. One final sweet goodbye.

'I have done my duty by my grandfather today. And, *matakia mou*, he would want me to be here with you.'

'He would?'

'My grandfather was a great believer in two things—duty and love.'

Her heart gave a little skip at his words, a skip she tried frantically to dampen.

'Please, Helios, don't say things like that. It isn't fair.'

He caught her chin and turned her face to look at him. 'How can the truth not be fair? You are my whole world. I love you.'

'Please, stop,' she beseeched, clutching at his shirt. 'Don't speak of love to me when you will be marrying Catalina—'

'I'm not marrying Catalina,' Helios interrupted, castigating himself for being foolish enough to believe Amy was a mind reader who would have known the truth from the minute she'd seen him from her plane window. 'The wedding is off.'

Her eyes widened into huge round orbs. 'It is? Since when?'

'Since about three hours ago, when I realised I couldn't live another day without you. Catalina and I had a talk.' Knowing Amy would be concerned for the Princess, he took pains to reassure her. 'She will be fine. She's as good a woman as you always told me, and I promise you we have her blessing.'

'But…' Nothing else came. Her mouth was opening and closing as if her tongue had forgotten how to form words.

He pressed his lips to hers, inhaling the warm, sweet breath he had believed he would never taste again.

'I love you,' he repeated, looking at her shocked face. 'It's you I want to marry. Just you. Only you.'

'I want that too. More than anything in the world.'

'Then why do you look so sad?'

'Because I know it can never be. You aren't allowed to marry a commoner.'

He took hold of her hand and pressed it to his chest. 'Listen to my heart,' he said quietly. 'I knew I had to find a wife when my grandfather was given his diagnosis, but I put it off and put it off because deep down I knew it would mean losing you. My heart has been beating for you from the very start.'

Her breath gave a tiny hitch.

'You asked me what I would have been if I hadn't been born heir to the throne and I had no good answer for you, because it wasn't something I had ever allowed myself to think about. The throne, my country…they were my life. I didn't expect love. My only hope for marriage was that it would be better than what my parents had. However it panned out I would do my duty and I would respect my wife. That was the most I hoped for. I didn't *want* love. I saw the way my father abused the power of my mother's love and I never wanted to have the power to inflict such hurt on a woman. That's why Catalina seemed so perfect—I thought she was emotionally cold.'

Amy shivered.

Helios tightened his hold and gently kissed her. 'I know I have the power to hurt you, *matakia mou*, and I swear on everything holy that I will never abuse it. But you need to understand one thing.'

'What's that?' she whispered.

'You have equal power to hurt me.'

'I do?'

'Living without you... It's been like living in an emotional dungeon. Cold and dark and without hope.' He brushed his thumb over her soft cheek. 'If spending the rest of my life with you means I have to relinquish the throne, then that's the price I'll pay and I'll pay it gladly.'

Her hold on his shirt tightening, her eyes wide and fearful, she said, 'But what about the throne? What will happen to it?'

'I don't know.' He laughed ruefully. 'Theseus is next in line. That's one of the things that struck me earlier—my grandparents raised *three* princes. It doesn't have to be me. We're all capable and worthy of taking the throne. Except Talos,' he added as an afterthought. 'Never mind that he's marrying a commoner too. He can be particularly fierce. He'll probably scare more people away from our country than attract them.'

She managed a painful chortle at his attempt at humour. 'But what if Theseus doesn't want it?'

'He probably *won't* want it,' he answered honestly. 'But he understands what it's like to be without the one you love. His fiancée has royal blood in her. It should be enough.'

'And if it isn't?'

'Then we will work something out. Whatever happens, I swear to you that we will be together until we take our dying breaths and that the Agon monarchy will remain intact. Have faith, *matakia mou*. And to prove it…'

Disentangling himself from her arms, he dug into his pocket and pulled out the object Pedro had set about retrieving a few short hours ago.

Dumbstruck, she simply stared at it as he displayed it to her.

'This, my love, belongs to you.' He took her trembling left hand, slid the ring onto her engagement finger, then kissed it. 'One day the eldest of our children will inherit it, and in turn they will pass it to the eldest of their children—

either to wear themselves upon marriage or for their wives to wear.'

'Our *children*?'

'You do want them, don't you?' he asked, suddenly anxious that he might have made one assumption too many. 'If you don't we can pass the ring to Theseus...'

'No, no—I *do* want your children,' she said. And then, like a cloud moving away from the sun, the fear left her eyes and a smile as wide as the sunset before them spread across her cheeks, lighting up her whole face. 'We're really going to be together?'

'Until death us do part.'

Such was the weight of her joy that when she threw herself into him he fell back onto the grass, taking her with him, and her overjoyed kisses as she straddled him filled him with more happiness than he had ever thought possible.

She was *his*. He was hers.

And as they lay on the grass, watching the orange sun make its final descent through the pink sky, he knew in his heart that the rest of his life would be filled with the glorious colours of this most beautiful of sunsets.

EPILOGUE

Six months later

THE RED DOME of the Aghia Sophia, the cathedral located in the exact central point between the Agon palace and the capital, Resina, gleamed as if it were burnt liquid gold under the autumn sky.

As Amy was taken through the cheering crowds on a horse-drawn carriage she turned her face upwards, letting the sun's rays warm her face, and sighed with contentment. Unlike many brides on their big day, she had no fear or apprehension whatsoever.

Beside her sat her father, who would be walking her down the aisle, and little Toby, proud as Punch to have been given the important role of ring bearer. In the carriage ahead of them sat her three bridesmaids: her soon-to-be sisters-in-law, Amalie and Jo, and Greta. Ahead of them were seven mounted military guards, in all their ceremonial attire, with the front rider holding the Kalliakis Royal Standard. More guards rode alongside the carriages, and there were a dozen at the rear.

It was pure pageantry at its finest. Triple the number of military guards were scheduled for a fortnight's time, when she and Helios would return to the cathedral to be crowned King and Queen of Agon.

In the sky were dozens of helicopters, sent from news outlets across the world to film the event.

Unbelievably she, Amy Green—a woman abandoned as a two-week-old baby by her birth mother, a woman who had never been quite sure of her place in the world—was going to be Queen of Agon.

Helios would be King. And it was the woman who'd abandoned her who'd made it all possible.

According to Helios, Theseus had turned the colour of puce when he'd sat his two brothers down and explained the situation to them. As Helios had suspected, Theseus had reluctantly agreed he would take the throne but only if all other avenues had first been explored.

Constitutional experts had been put on the case, to no avail, until Talos had come up with the bright idea of changing the constitution, rightly pointing out it had been changed numerous times before.

A meeting with the Agon senate had been arranged, and there the president, who, like all the members of the senate, was sympathetic to the Crown Prince's plight, had murmured about how much easier it would be to bring about the constitutional change if the bride were of Agon blood…

A referendum had taken place. Of the ninety per cent turnout, ninety-three per cent had voted for changing the constitution to allow a person of non-royal blood to marry into the royal family, provided that she was of Agon blood.

And now, as the carriage pulled up at the front of the cathedral, where the cheers from the crowd were deafening, Amy was helped down. She stepped carefully, so as not to trip over the fifteen-foot train of her ivory silk dress, handmade by Queen Rhea's personal designer, Natalia.

How she loved her dress, with its spaghetti straps and the rounded neck that skimmed her cleavage, the flared skirt that was as far from the traditional meringue shape as could be. Simpler in form and design than both Queen Rhea's dress and Helios's mother's dress, it was utterly perfect for her. And it was lucky she had insisted on something simpler considering they'd had to expand the waistline at the last fitting, to take into account the swelling of her stomach…

She and Helios had taken the decision a couple of months ago for Amy to come off the contraceptive pill, both of them figuring that it would take a good few months for the hormones to get out of her system. The hope had been that she would conceive after their coronation.

Whoops.

A month after taking her last pill Amy's breasts had suddenly grown in size. Their baby—the new heir to the throne—was due in six months, something they had decided not to make public until after their coronation. Naturally half the palace knew about it.

Greta had been given Corinna's job at the museum and was thoroughly enjoying bossing Amy about. Amy had gone back to curating King Astraeus's exhibition and then, when the exhibition had closed, she'd taken on the role of museum tour guide. It was a job she would be able to fit around the royal duties she would have to take on when she was crowned Queen.

Helios still thought it appropriate to give bloodthirsty Agon history lessons to children in the dungeons.

In all, everything had worked out perfectly, as if the stars had aligned for them.

Jo stepped forward to adjust Amy's veil, having to stretch to accommodate her own swollen stomach, which was fast resembling a beach ball, and then it was time.

When her arm was held tightly in her father's, the doors of the cathedral were thrown open, the music started and Amy took the first step towards the rest of her life.

The congregation rose as one, every head turning to stare. The first face she saw was that of Princess Catalina, who, as gracious as ever, smiled at Amy with both her lips and her eyes.

When the press had bombarded her with questions about Helios and Amy's marriage her statement of support for them had been heartfelt and touching.

Surely somewhere in this packed cathedral stood a prince in need of a beautiful, elegant princess to make his own?

In the back row was the woman who had made all this happen—Neysa Soukis, there with her husband, and their son, Leander. It was amazing how the thought of being Queen Mother had spurred Neysa to recognise Amy as her child with enthusiasm and thus proclaim her a child of Agon blood. No doubt Neysa had imagined this moment many times, had thought she would be sitting in the front row of the congregation.

Alas, Neysa had soon learned that the only place she had in Amy's life was as a name on a piece of paper. Elaine—her mum, the woman who had raised and loved her—would be the officially recognised Queen Mother.

And, thinking of her mum, there she stood in the front row, beautiful in a pea-green skirt suit and an enormous hat, beaming with pride. Next to her stood Amy's *real* brothers, Neil and

Danny, with identical grins on their faces. Both of them had been fit to burst with pride when Helios had appointed them as his ushers. Their wives had a dazed, 'someone pinch me to prove this is really happening' look about them.

And best of all, standing at the front, beside the altar, his brothers by his side, stood Helios; her lover and her best friend all rolled into one.

The three Princes were dressed in their military uniforms: the Kalliakis livery complete with sashes. They all looked magnificent, like three benevolent giants.

Helios might not be able to see her face through her veil, but she could see his, and see the full beard he'd grown especially for her. The expression in his eyes made every step she took closer to him feel as if she were bouncing on the moon.

When she reached him Helios took her hand, and together they knelt at the altar to pledge their lives, fidelity and love to each other for ever.

They were pledges neither of them would ever break.

* * * * *

MILLS & BOON®
Large Print – June 2016

Leonetti's Housekeeper Bride
Lynne Graham

The Surprise De Angelis Baby
Cathy Williams

Castelli's Virgin Widow
Caitlin Crews

The Consequence He Must Claim
Dani Collins

Helios Crowns His Mistress
Michelle Smart

Illicit Night with the Greek
Susanna Carr

The Sheikh's Pregnant Prisoner
Tara Pammi

Saved by the CEO
Barbara Wallace

Pregnant with a Royal Baby!
Susan Meier

A Deal to Mend Their Marriage
Michelle Douglas

Swept into the Rich Man's World
Katrina Cudmore

0516 Rom LP

MILLS & BOON®
Large Print – July 2016

The Italian's Ruthless Seduction
Miranda Lee

Awakened by Her Desert Captor
Abby Green

A Forbidden Temptation
Anne Mather

A Vow to Secure His Legacy
Annie West

Carrying the King's Pride
Jennifer Hayward

Bound to the Tuscan Billionaire
Susan Stephens

Required to Wear the Tycoon's Ring
Maggie Cox

The Greek's Ready-Made Wife
Jennifer Faye

Crown Prince's Chosen Bride
Kandy Shepherd

Billionaire, Boss...Bridegroom?
Kate Hardy

Married for Their Miracle Baby
Soraya Lane

MILLS & BOON®

Why shop at millsandboon.co.uk?

Each year, thousands of romance readers find their perfect read at millsandboon.co.uk. That's because we're passionate about bringing you the very best romantic fiction. Here are some of the advantages of shopping at www.millsandboon.co.uk:

* **Get new books first**—you'll be able to buy your favourite books one month before they hit the shops

* **Get exclusive discounts**—you'll also be able to buy our specially created monthly collections, with up to 50% off the RRP

* **Find your favourite authors**—latest news, interviews and new releases for all your favourite authors and series on our website, plus ideas for what to try next

* **Join in**—once you've bought your favourite books, don't forget to register with us to rate, review and join in the discussions

Visit **www.millsandboon.co.uk**
for all this and more today!